"I would marry you."

Marissa looked half afraid. "That isn't funny."

"No one said I was joking."

"You don't even know my name."

No, Alex guessed he didn't. Nor did she know his. He'd been known to be impulsive, but it took a certain kind of brashness to propose to a woman when you didn't even know her name.

But he said it again. "I would marry you."

She laughed and got out of his truck. Well, maybe he'd been wrong. He was, after all, Alex Palermo. In his experience, women wanted to date him but they didn't want to marry him. To the people in Bluebonnet Springs, he was a Palermo. On the bull-riding circuit he was a little bit wild, and not the guy anyone wanted to settle down with.

Not only that, but most women didn't accept proposals from strangers who picked them up on the side of the road.

Besides, she was out of his league. She knew it. He knew it. But he couldn't help but admire her.

Brenda Minton lives in the Ozarks with her husband, children, cats, dogs and strays. She is a pastor's wife, Sunday-school teacher, coffee addict and sleep deprived. Not in that order. Her dream to be an author for Harlequin started somewhere in the pages of a romance novel about a young American woman stranded in a Spanish castle. Her dreams came true, and twenty-plus books later, she is an author hoping to inspire young girls to dream.

Visit the Author Profile page at Harlequin.com for more titles

The Rancher's Christmas Bride

Brenda Minton

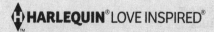

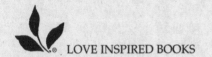

Recycling programs
for this product may
not exist in your area.

LOVE INSPIRED BOOKS

ISBN-13: 978-0-373-89971-5

The Rancher's Christmas Bride

www.Harlequin.com

Printed in U.S.A.

And we know that God causes everything to work together for the good of those who love God and are called according to His purpose for them.
—*Romans* 8:28

To Josh and Brooke, for pitching in and making everything so much easier for me. I'm blessed to have such amazing kids. And to my editor, Melissa Endlich, because she's awesome.

Chapter One

When memories crashed in on Alex Palermo, he drove. He never thought about a destination. He only knew that if he rolled down his truck windows, played some cowboy country on the radio and prayed, the memories would fade and so would the guilt. The praying part happened to be a new addition to the process. Pastor Matthews of the Bluebonnet Community Church had insisted he try it.

They'd joked that real men can eat quiche. Real men can pray. They can even cry every once in a while. As long as it didn't become habit. They'd fist-bumped and joked over that.

On a cool day in December, Texas Hill Country wasn't at its warmest. But the breeze coming through the open windows of his truck helped to clear his mind. He'd been doing really well, but tonight, maybe because it was almost ten years to the day since he'd killed his father, the memories had resurfaced with a vengeance.

No, he hadn't really killed his father. Deep down he knew that he hadn't. But for years he'd told himself he was responsible for the death of Jesse Palermo. In reality, alcohol and a mean bull had killed Alex's father.

Earlier, standing in the arena where his father had drawn a bull rope—and his last breath—Alex had been hard put to remember that it hadn't been his fault his dad had gotten on that bull.

The tires of his truck hummed on the pavement. He took a deep breath and turned up the radio. As if he could outrun the pain.

A few miles out of Bluebonnet Springs, he hit the brakes. Because either he'd gone crazy, or ahead of him, on the shoulder of the road, was a woman in a wedding dress. The last thing he wanted was a bride, even someone else's bride. His common sense told him to keep on driving.

Common sense told him that he had enough problems of his own without getting tied up in someone else's hard times. He'd taken off driving in the hopes of outrunning some of those problems.

Unfortunately he'd never been good at listening. His twin, Marcus, always accused him of being the good twin. He didn't know if he'd agree with that, but he supposed he must have a chivalrous side. He pulled to the shoulder just ahead and got out of his truck. The woman was definitely real. And wearing a wedding dress. As if on cue, it started to rain. Steady, big drops. The kind of rain that danced across the pavement and soaked a person's clothing.

"Need a lift?" he asked, hoping they could get back in the dry warmth of his truck soon.

Better yet, she could tell him she had a ride already on the way to pick her up. But a bride without a groom? That didn't exactly spell wedding bells and happily-ever-after.

"I'm fine." She said it with her chin raised a notch, even as the rain picked up pace. He was losing objectivity because that little lift of her chin showed some pride and big eyes that rivaled the stormy sky.

"Ri-i-i-ght." He said it slowly. Did he point out to her that she was miles from anywhere, wearing a wedding dress and standing in the rain?

"You can go on. I know where I'm going."

He looked around, at the open fields, pastures full of cattle and nothing else. He glanced back at her and grinned, because they both knew she was bluffing.

"I know we're taught from the time we're little not to get in the car with a stranger. But I think even your mama would want you to get in out of the rain."

Hands up so she could see them, he took a step toward her.

She reached for the bag slung over her shoulder. "Don't come any closer. I'm armed."

He glanced at the bag and the object pointing through the thin cotton. "With a high-heeled shoe?"

"I'm warning you." She issued the command with a startling amount of conviction as rain poured down from the steel-gray sky. She was a tiny thing with a pixie face and a massive amount of brown hair piled on top of her head.

Rain dripped down her face and she swiped it away with her shoulder. That chivalrous side of him kicked into gear. He jerked off his jean jacket and held it out to her. She eyed it the way a stray kitten eyed a bowl of milk, but didn't take it.

"Well, I'm not really worried you'll shoot me with a shoe." He grinned as he said it, hoping to put her at ease. "But I do think we're both in trouble if we don't get out of this rain. I'm not going to hurt you, I just want to get you off the road."

The rain picked up and he saw her shiver. Her feet were bare. So were her arms. She took another swipe at the water dripping down her face. She eyed the jacket and his truck.

"Listen, we could stand here all night or I can just literally pick you up and put you in my truck." He did not want to do that. She looked like the kind of female that once a man had her in his arms, he'd want to hold her forever.

He didn't do forever.

For a full minute she stood there facing him, then she nodded, giving in. He hurried ahead of her to open the passenger door of the truck. As she struggled to get her skirts under control, he took her hand and helped her in.

That hand was like a frail bird's, cold and fine-boned. He held it gently, afraid he'd hurt her.

"Are we on the way to the church? Or do you have somewhere else you'd like me to take you?" he asked as he climbed behind the wheel of his truck.

Huddled in the seat, her teeth chattered. He turned up the heat.

"Do you know Dan Wilson?" she asked, hugging herself for warmth.

"Yeah, I know Dan."

"Could you take me to his house?"

He tried again to give her his jacket. This time she took it, sniffing at the collar before settling it over her bare arms.

"It's clean," he said, a little defensively.

"I know, I just…" She shrugged a bit and

looked sheepish. "I'm sorry. It's been a long day. If you could take me to Dan's…"

"I can, but do you know what you're getting yourself into?"

She gave him a puzzled look. "No, I guess not."

"Dan isn't the most pleasant guy in the world. He's been sick and that's made him extra cranky."

"I'm his granddaughter."

He had pulled onto the road so he shot her a quick look. "Seriously? I mean, not that you can't be. But I didn't know Dan even had a granddaughter."

"He hasn't seen my mom since she was a little girl. I tried to get him to come to the wedding…" She let the words trail off as her gaze slid to the window. A delicate finger brushed across her cheek.

Tears. He'd never been good with tears. He had two sisters and fortunately neither of them was the type to cry. The Palermo siblings had learned the hard way that tears didn't help. In fact, sometimes tears made it worse.

His dad hadn't invented the warning "Do you want me to give you something to cry about?" but he'd definitely put action to the words. He'd put the words into action the night he'd locked Lucy in the tack room of their barn. He had

put the words into action the night he'd punched
Marcus in the throat. They'd all learned not to
cry and they'd learned not to tell.

But that had nothing to do with now and the
lady sitting beside him wanting a ride to Dan's.

"None of my business, but does Dan know
you're coming? I don't think he'd take kindly
to a surprise family reunion."

From the look on her face, a grim mixture of
worry and sadness, she wasn't amused by his
poor attempt at humor. Some things just weren't
that funny. And a bride that was walking down
a back road, still in her wedding dress, pretending a shoe was a weapon? He guessed she'd had
a pretty rough day.

The road was bumpy, but as they bounced
along he managed to open the glove compart-
ment and pull out a box of tissues.

"I'm not going to cry," she insisted. But a few
tears trickled down her cheeks.

"I guess I don't have a right to ask what happened. But if you need to talk, I'm all ears." He
glanced in the mirror. "Seriously, have you ever
seen ears this big?"

She glanced at him and burst into watery laughter, shaking her head as she surveyed his ears.

"They aren't *that* big," she countered. At least
he'd made her laugh. He'd always been good for
a laugh. And not much more.

"He picked the caterer," she said quietly into the darkened interior of the truck. Her voice was soft, kind of sweet.

The windshield wipers clicked as they swept back and forth, and Chris LeDoux was singing "Cadillac Ranch." Alex cleared his throat and shot her another quick look.

"Who picked the caterer? You mean you let him decide what to feed the guests and you're upset about that? I think you'd need a bigger reason to walk out on a wedding."

She shook her head vehemently. "No, he picked the caterer."

He pulled to the side of the road because he couldn't focus on the road and a conversation that seemed important. She fingered the sleeve of the jean jacket and her gaze slid to the window.

"He picked the caterer," she said with meaning. "Not the chicken or the beef—the caterer. He picked her. Over me."

She pinched the bridge of her nose, closed her eyes and breathed. The tears disappeared but they'd left streaks down her cheeks. They'd left marks, the way this wedding would leave marks, he knew with certainty.

Another reason he was single and planned to stay that way. People had a tendency to hurt one another. His dad had hurt everyone in his path. His mom had walked out on her own children.

He shifted and pulled back onto the road, trying to find the right thing to say. A few minutes later he drove into Dan Wilson's driveway.

"I'm sorry," he told her, knowing his apology wasn't the one that mattered. She'd been left at the altar by the man she had planned to spend her life with. He could tell her hard lessons about being let down by people who should have cared, but she didn't need to hear it from him.

He'd let down people, too. He'd let down his siblings. He'd let down his best friend. He guessed he'd let down himself a few times, too. That made him the last person who could really help the woman sitting next to him in the dim light of his truck. He reached to turn down the radio and told himself it didn't mean a thing. This moment would pass, like so many moments in his life. For these few minutes, though, maybe he could be her hero, the person she could count on.

"He was a fool. If he picked the caterer, he didn't deserve you." He parked next to Dan's old farm truck.

She leaned across the truck in a rustle of white satin and lace and kissed his cheek. "Thank you. I don't even know your name, but thank you."

He held out his hand. "Alex Palermo, at your service."

She took his hand and again he was surprised

by the way it felt, as if he should cherish the moment a little longer. "Marissa Walker."

The rain was steady now and the light of early evening had given way to darkness. She peered through the windshield and frowned. "Is that my grandfather's home?"

Alex glanced away from the bride sitting next to him and nodded as he looked at the little camper, hay bales stacked underneath to keep out the winter wind. "That's Dan's place."

"He lives in a camper?"

"For as long as I've known him. He's always been ornery and he's always lived in this camper. Don't let it fool you. He's one of the best horse trainers in the country and he raises some mighty fine Angus cattle."

A gunshot split the night, ending the conversation. The woman sitting next to him screamed. "He's shooting at us!"

"Nah," he said with a grin. "He's just warning us to get off his land."

Marissa couldn't help it; she cowered in the seat, close to the cowboy. He was a stranger, but at the moment he was the only thing she had to hold on to. The day was catching up with her. She'd been awake since sunrise, because it was her wedding day and there'd been so much to get done. And then she'd stood in the dressing room of the wedding venue waiting for Aidan. And waiting. Until he sent the text that he was on his way to Hawaii. With Linda, the caterer. Unable to face her family and friends, she'd taken off with the limousine, leaving her mom a note that she needed time.

The limousine had broken down and the driver had told her he was done. The tow truck would take him back to the city and she was on her own unless she wanted to go to Austin.

And now this. Her grandfather was a madman with a gun.

The cowboy sitting next to her rolled down his window and leaned out. "Dan, stop shooting. You're a little shaky these days and you might accidentally shoot someone."

"Is that you, Alex?"

"Yeah, it's me. And you don't usually shoot at me when I pull up."

"Cattle thieves have hauled off three of my best heifers, Alex. I ain't taking no chances."

"Yeah, but I'm your neighbor, not a cattle thief. And I've got your granddaughter in the truck with me. This isn't the best way to introduce yourself."

That was her cue. Marissa got out and walked tentatively through the dark and the mud to the front of the truck, where headlights illuminated the trailer and the man standing on the rickety porch. She glanced around, looking for the cowboy, and he was there, joining her. He grinned and winked and she felt as if he was her lifeline for the time being. A stranger with dark flashing eyes, dimpled cheeks and a flirty smile. A black cowboy hat covered his head but she thought she saw dark curls peek out from beneath.

His hand touched her back, between her shoulder blades, giving her strength to move forward.

"I'm Marissa. I'm your granddaughter."

Her grandfather leaned against the porch as a fit of coughing hit. She wanted to tell him they'd be better off inside, but she wasn't sure yet that it was true. Or even that he'd let her inside. Her grandmother had walked out on him, taking his only child, Marissa's mom. He probably wasn't going to feel too charitable to his only grandchild.

"I thought you were getting married today," he said, surprising her. "What are you doing here?"

"I wanted to meet you." She couldn't very well tell him that she was twenty-six and she'd basically run away from home. That she'd run from a wedding that would have been the social embarrassment of the decade.

"You wanted to meet me?" He barked out a harsh laugh. "On your wedding day? Where's your groom?"

"Hawaii."

"Shouldn't you be with him?" he asked, his voice softening a bit.

"I would have been if he hadn't left with the caterer."

He sighed. "That's too bad. But that doesn't explain why you're here."

She bit down on her lip, unsure of what she should say. "I need a place to stay."

"I'm sure you have a home and parents to go to."

"Dan, it's just for a night," Alex Palermo said with a confident tone as he winked at Marissa.

She hadn't said a thing about it being for just one night.

Dan's hand was on the doorknob of the camper. "I don't have an extra bed. And I don't think a princess like her, in a dress that cost more than this camper, is going to want to stay here."

"I *do* want to stay." She took a few cautious steps forward.

"You don't have to," Alex said out of the corner of his mouth. "We can find somewhere else for you to stay."

"Didn't you hear the girl, Alex? She's my granddaughter. She's welcome to sleep on the couch. Tonight." Her grandfather started to take a step inside but he wobbled a bit.

Alex hurried up the steps and steadied the older man. Marissa watched, unsure.

"Dan, are you okay?" Alex asked.

"I'm fine." Marissa's grandfather shook loose from the hand that steadied him. "A little light-headed from this cold. Get on in out of the rain, girl."

"You're sure about this?" Alex asked again.

"I'm sure," she answered. Nervous or not, she was staying.

"Nobody's asking if *I'm* sure," her grandfather grumbled but he pushed the door open and motioned her inside. "Go on, Alex. We're fine. You can come by tomorrow and check on her."

Alex gave her one last look and left, walking down the rickety steps and across the muddy yard to his truck. She watched him go and then she stepped inside the camper and the door closed them in.

She heard the truck start, and her last chance to escape was driving off into the rain-soaked night, leaving her with a less-than-welcoming stranger. She peeked out the window, saw brake lights on the truck and smiled, because, unlike her groom, he wasn't leaving without a second thought. And it felt good to know that a stranger, someone who didn't have to care, did.

Chapter Two

Something heavy stretched out on Marissa's legs. She tried to move and it growled long and low. She froze, peeking up at the bloodhound that stretched across her. The movement brought another soft noise from the animal—it wasn't quite threatening, but was more of a warning growl. She looked up at the ceiling as another wave of something that felt like grief washed over her.

Today she should have woken up in Hawaii. She should be Mrs. Aidan Dean. Instead she was on her grandfather's couch somewhere outside Bluebonnet Springs, Texas. Sometime in the night she'd decided she would never again play the fool. She would be stronger. More independent. She wouldn't back down or give up. Aidan had hurt her badly. But he hadn't broken her.

At least her grandfather had given her a place

to stay the night. Last night, after Alex Palermo had left, they'd eaten bologna sandwiches in silence as he watched a game show. After the show ended he'd declared it bedtime. He'd tossed her a quilt and a pillow before he headed to his room. At the door he'd warned her about Bub, without telling her who Bub might be.

She guessed that Bub was the dog stretched out next to her.

"Get down," she insisted. Bub just sprawled a little more and rested his head on her belly. "No, really, I don't like dogs. Go," she muttered, moving her legs. Bub growled again but nestled in closer.

She closed her eyes to regroup and must have dozed off again. A rooster crowed, something banged loudly against the roof and she jumped. Bub rolled off the sofa. He landed with a thud, shook his entire body and stared at her with meaningful contempt in his sad eyes. Marissa ignored him as she got to her feet and looked around.

In the light of day, the camper was small and cluttered. Magazines were stacked on tables. The kitchen was just a tiny corner with a minifridge and stove, a single sink and a few cabinets. A mirror hung on a closet door. She took a cautious peek at the woman in the reflection. The woman looking back at her had long hair that hung in a tangled knot. The wedding dress, a monstrous creation with too many sequins and ruffles, was wrinkled and stained. She didn't know herself. Maybe once, a long time ago, she'd known what she wanted. She might have had her own dreams. But over the years she'd lost sight of the dreamer, the achiever, and she'd fought hard to become the person her parents wanted her to be. She'd lost herself.

When she left the wedding venue and headed for Bluebonnet Springs yesterday, that might have been an awakening. A rediscovery of the girl she'd left behind.

Looking back, she realized nothing about this wedding had been her choice, her style. The wedding venue, the dress, the flowers and the cake had all been picked by her mother. Guilt had robbed her of the ability to speak up for herself. She was her mother's only child. This would have been her mom's only wedding to plan. And on every last thing, Marissa had conceded to her mother's desires.

Because of guilt.

Looking at her hair, she realized that she'd been giving up pieces of herself for a very long time. And now, because of Aidan, it was time to start taking back some of her independence.

She headed for the kitchen and rummaged through drawers until she found what she was looking for. She pulled out the clips and pins from her hair, then grabbed it up, leaned forward and cut it with scissors she'd found in a junk drawer.

The sound of scissors slicing through hair brought her back to reality. She looked at the long chunk of hair in her hand and straightened to look in the mirror at the ghastly sight.

"What have I done?"

Next to her the dog whined. She glanced down at the beast stretched out at her feet. He looked up at her with soulful eyes and six inches of drool hanging from his mouth.

"Did I really do that?" she asked him. In answer he put his head on his paws and closed his eyes. Of course he didn't have an opinion. She returned her attention to the rather uneven layers of hair.

She snipped away the longer pieces, shortening her hair by another two inches. She looked in the mirror and winced. Her hair was now just above her shoulders. It wasn't the best cut in the world but it felt good to be rid of the weight. She brushed it out with her fingers and then tossed the long locks she'd cut in the trash and dropped the scissors back in the drawer.

Now to find her grandfather. She opened the front door and was greeted by a sunny December day. There was a hint of chill in the air and the smell of wet earth. And no sign of Dan. She stepped back inside, leaving the door open a crack.

The camper wasn't big, maybe thirty feet in length. She walked to the hallway and peered into the empty bathroom.

"Dan? Are you here?" She took another cautious step. "Dan?"

And then she heard the coughing, the same as the previous evening, almost as if he couldn't catch his breath. She knocked on the closed bedroom door.

"Dan? Are you okay?"

The coughing fit lasted a few more seconds. "I'm fine. Can't you leave a man in peace?"

"Not if he sounds like he might need help," she said through the closed door. "Do you need help?"

"No, I don't need help. Not unless you plan to feed livestock for me." Through the thin door she heard a raspy chuckle.

"Okay. I think I can do that."

"You don't know a cow from a bull." He began coughing again.

"Do you need a doctor?"

"Call your folks and tell them to come get you," he said at the end of the spell, his breathing sounding off, even through the door.

"I texted them yesterday but my phone didn't charge last night."

"Deliver me from nosy relatives and do-gooders," he grumbled. But she thought he sounded pleased. Or maybe she wanted him to be pleased.

"You rest. I'll figure out the difference between a cow and a bull."

"Don't get too close to that bull or you'll be on the business end of his horns. City gals. Land sakes, they drive a man nuts."

"I'll yell if I need help." She looked down at the wedding dress. She guessed it wouldn't do any good to ask for clothes.

As she headed out the front door and down the steps, careful to avoid loose boards, something red and winged came flying at her. She jumped off the porch and ran but it kept up the chase. The dog began barking and joined the fray. Chickens scattered, squawking in protest.

The crazy thing jumped at her, claws ripping at her dress, and a vicious beak tried to grab hold. She headed for the beat-up old truck parked to the side of the driveway, and when the doors wouldn't open, she climbed in the back, the dress tangling around her legs. She fell in a heap of white, but then she scrambled to her feet, grabbing a rake that had been left in the bed of the truck.

A truck eased down the drive and stopped a

dozen feet from where she stood. Through the window, even with the glare of early morning sun, she could see the cowboy from the previous evening. His wide grin was unmistakable.

The rooster must have known she'd been distracted. He flew at her again. She was ready this time and gave him a good smack with the rake. He made a stupid chicken noise as he fell to the ground, squawking and fluttering his wings.

Alex Palermo got out of his truck, shaking his head and smirking just a little. She probably looked a sight, standing there in the bed of a truck wearing her wedding dress. He didn't look like he'd slept on a sofa. No, he looked rested. As he took off his cowboy hat, she saw his hair was dark and curly. His ears really were a little too big. It was good to know he wasn't perfect. He was compact with broad shoulders, wore jeans that fit easy on his trim waist and had a grin that would melt a girl's heart. Any girl but her.

Her heart was off-limits. Out of order. No longer available.

"It looks like you've killed Dan's rooster," Alex glanced at the rooster and then raised his gaze to hers. "Want down from there?"

She peeked over the side of the truck, where the rooster had regained his footing. "The rooster looks very much alive to me."

He flashed a smile, revealing those dimples

again. "Yeah, I was teasing. He's a little stunned. I doubt he's ever been knocked out with a rake."

"Stop," she warned. "That rooster had it coming. And the dog is going down next."

"What did Bub ever do to you?" He held out a hand for her. "Come on down now, you'll be fine. I'll protect you."

But who would protect her from all of that cowboy charm? He was cute and he knew how to make a girl feel rescued without making her feel weak. She took his hand and managed to climb over the tailgate of the truck without getting tangled up in the massive white skirts. If she'd had her choice she would have picked a slim-fitting dress that didn't overwhelm her five-foot frame.

"My grandfather is sick," she told him once she was on the ground.

"Dan has emphysema," Alex explained and then he held out a bag. "I guess someone will be here to get you today, but I borrowed some clothes from my sister. They'll be a little bit big on you but I'd imagine you'd like to get out of that dress."

"Thank you." She held the bag and looked back at the camper. "I told him I'd feed his livestock."

His eyes twinkled. "Did you now? And do you know how to feed livestock?"

"I'll figure it out."

"I don't doubt that a bit. But I'll help you. I usually try to check on Dan every few days, since he hasn't had anyone else."

Her grandfather didn't have anyone. Of course he didn't. She hadn't even known about him until her grandmother passed away the previous summer. There were family secrets and hurt feelings. She got all of that. But Dan deserved family. He needed family.

"Oh, city girl, I wouldn't get that look in my eyes if I were you."

She glanced up at the man standing in front of her, watching her with his steady gaze. "What look?"

"The look that says you think Old Dan needs rescuing. He won't take kindly to that."

"But he…"

Alex held up a hand. "You just showed up and he has pride. He isn't going to let you come in here and start prodding him into submission because you're a granddaughter with a need to make up for lost time."

"But he's sick," she sputtered. "And I *am* his granddaughter."

"Right, I get that. I'll give you some advice, before you ride in there on a white horse. Let Dan think he's helping you."

Her indignation died a quick death. "Oh."

He pointed to the bag of clothes. "Go change and I'll wait for you."

For the first time she took a good look at the place her grandfather called home. The land was flat to a point and then it met rolling, tree-covered hills. The fences sagged and the barn looked as if it was at least a century old. The camper sat in the middle of it all, a relic from decades past. Behind that was a chicken pen, the door open and the rooster now inside getting himself a drink of water but still watching her with serious intent.

"Go on," he said, and patted her shoulder. "I've learned that life has these little moments. I guess we learn from them when we can and we survive."

She saw something in him she hadn't noticed before. There was laughter on the surface, but in his dark eyes she saw pain. For a moment it was so intense, that flash of sadness, she wanted to comfort him. She shook free and stepped back. His easy smile was back in place and he winked, making her think she'd imagined it all.

Alex scrounged around in the shed, found the chicken feed and scooped out a can. As he exited the building, Marissa came out of the camper. She was dressed in his older sister's—Lucy's—jeans and a T-shirt she'd tied at the waist. Probably to keep it from hanging to her knees. The jeans were tucked into the boots he'd borrowed from his little sister, Maria.

He wondered if he should comment on her hair. Having been raised with two sisters, he kind of doubted it. Even though it was a little short and uneven, he liked it.

"So, you might not be a country girl, but dressed like that you could fool some people."

"Because I put on jeans and boots?" She shook her head and kept walking.

If he had to guess, that fast walk of hers was intended to help her outrun an argument with her grandfather. He paused for a few seconds, and sure enough the door of the camper flew open and Dan, in overalls, muck boots and a straw hat, appeared. His gray hair stuck out from beneath the hat and his face was scruffy with a few days' growth of gray whiskers.

"I don't need no pity from long lost relatives," Dan squawked, sounding a lot like that bad-tempered rooster of his. "Now call your folks and tell them to come get you. After all these years…"

He had a coughing fit and didn't finish. And even with the tongue lashing, his granddaughter hightailed it back to his side and told him to take it easy. She might be a city girl but she had a determined side.

Alex didn't want to like her too much. In his experience, women like her didn't last in his world. And they were too expensive for his bank account. It didn't matter what he told himself about her being a city girl, or his bank account or any of the other mental objections he might have; he liked her.

A woman like her, if she stayed around long enough, could make a guy start thinking about forever. Even if he hadn't planned on having those thoughts. Ever. "I'm asking you to let me stay because I need a little time before I go back and face the embarrassment." She looked at her grandfather as determined as that old rooster had been. "Just a week or two. Please."

Dan reached into his pocket for an inhaler. After a few puffs, he shoved it in the front pocket of his bibs and gave his granddaughter a once-over.

"Nope." He went on down the steps, holding tight to the rail. "You call your folks and you go on back to Dallas. I don't need a keeper. And you don't need to hide from what happened."

"But…" She followed him. "I could help you out around here."

Dan shook his head as he took the can of chicken feed from Alex. "I don't need help. I'm just fine."

"Dan, just let us feed for you today," Alex

offered. But at this point, if he had any sense, he'd hightail it back to his place and take care of his own life instead of wading knee-deep into Dan's. "Give your granddaughter the chance to be a farm girl for a few days. She's all dressed up for the part. Might as well introduce her to country life. Maybe we'll even take a ride over to Essie's for lunch. My treat."

Dan looked skeptical, but even he seemed to know when to give in. He handed over the feed can and gave his granddaughter a sharp look. "Don't be abusing my rooster. He'll remember that and he'll be waiting to get back at you."

"He's a rooster," she said. "I doubt roosters plot vengeance."

"Just you wait," was his grumbled response as he headed back to the trailer. "I'm holding you to lunch, Palermo. You're buying."

"What do we do now?" the woman at his side asked Alex as they headed for Dan's old farm truck.

Alex unlocked her door and opened it. "Well, we feed Dan's cattle. In the summer he had plenty of grass, but this time of year we feed hay and grain. In years past that would have been more of a job than it is now. Dan's been selling off some cattle recently. I've actually been a little worried about him."

"Do you think he's okay? I mean…" She hesitated and then got in the truck. "Dementia?"

He got in and turned the key, knowing it would take a few attempts to get the old truck started. Dan had a sedan he kept parked in a carport behind the camper, but he claimed it didn't have a battery.

"No, I don't think he has dementia," he answered as the truck roared to life. "His health isn't the best but I think it's more. Something seems off and he won't say much about it."

"If he'll let me stay, maybe I can figure it out."

Alex thought the best thing she could do was head on back to Dallas. Dan's old camper suited him but it wasn't the life she was used to. Not that he knew about her life or what she was used to. But he guessed she didn't know what it was like to live in an old piece of metal when the wind blew hard from the north.

"I don't think he's going to let you stay," Alex told her as they drove toward the barn.

"Have you always known him?" she asked after he'd opened the gate and they'd driven through.

"All my life. He's always been here."

"So you grew up in Bluebonnet?"

He stopped the truck at the feed trough and got out. She followed, watching him, then watching the cattle heading their way. She moved to his side and stayed close as he tossed a feed sack over his shoulder, pulled the string to unseal the bag and poured it out, starting at one end of the trough.

"Did you?" she asked as he went back for the second bag of grain.

"Yeah, I grew up here."

"You don't sound happy about that."

"Because I'm busy and you're asking a lot of questions." Questions about growing up were his least favorite. There were too many bad memories attached to his childhood in Bluebonnet. Not because of the town but because his father had tarnished childhood for Alex and his siblings in a way that should have been against the law. It probably was against the law.

"Do you have siblings other than your sister?" she asked.

He pulled off his hat, swiped a hand across his brow and shook his head. "You know a guy for five seconds and suddenly you need his life story."

She started to protest but he stopped her. Holding his hand up to quiet her, he studied the cattle that were heading across the field. His attention shifted to the slightly damp ground. And tire tracks.

"What's wrong?" Marissa asked as she moved to stand next to him.

He pointed to the tracks in the soft earth. "Someone has been out here. On four-wheelers. And I might be wrong but there seems to be a couple of cows missing. I wouldn't usually notice that about Dan's herd, but he had two black baldies that looked ready to drop their calves any day. And they're gone. I'll ask Dan if I need to go look for them. It's possible they're off having their calves. But I don't know who would have been out here with an ATV."

"Black baldy?" she asked with narrowed eyes and her nose scrunched up.

"A black cow with a white face."

Her mouth formed an O. "Maybe he sold them?"

"Yeah, maybe."

He tossed the empty sacks and headed for the truck. "We'll ask him when we get back. And then I'll head to my place. I've got to get some work done before more rain hits."

"Work? Do you have another job, other than ranching?"

Another question. He motioned her into the truck. "I used to be a bull rider. Now I ranch and I'm starting a tractor-and-equipment-repair business. I also own bucking bulls." He got in the truck and cranked the engine. "What about you?"

"I teach kindergarten." She said it with a soft

smile but also with a little bit of sadness that he didn't like. She looked like the type of person who walked on sunshine and never had a bad day. But that's what he got for judging a book by its pretty cover.

Everyone had bad days. Most people had secrets or a past they didn't want to talk about. Those were the hard facts of life. He tried to stay out of other people's business and leave them to their own past, their own secrets.

Marissa Walker caused a man to forget those simple rules for an uninvolved life. Rule 1: don't ask personal questions.

They were nearing the gate and he slowed. "Why don't you open that gate for me?"

She climbed out of the truck and pulled on the gate until she had it open. A couple of times she had to stop and tug up on the jeans Lucy had loaned her. He swallowed a grin as she got back in the truck.

"I hope you enjoyed that," she muttered.

"I did." He leaned over to brush her cheek. "You had something on your face."

And just like that the humor died, and he was face-to-face with the greatest temptation of his life, a woman who just last night had sat in his truck and cried. A woman who wouldn't be around long enough to know left from right when it came to Bluebonnet.

He leaned back in the seat and put his hands on the steering wheel of the old truck. The clutch was sticky and the gears grinded a bit. It was familiar, and right now he needed familiar.

As they pulled up to Dan's camper, his passenger let out a soft gasp and reached for the door handle before he could get the truck stopped.

"Hey, at least let me stop before you…"

She was already out of the truck, the door wide-open. He hit the emergency brake and jumped out because Dan was leaning against the side of the camper and he didn't look too good. Alex remembered those praying lessons the pastor had been giving him, because this looked like a moment to pray for some help, to pray for an old man to take another breath.

"Dan, are you okay? Here, let me help you sit down." Marissa had an arm around him but he was fighting her off.

"I can get myself to the house." He leaned, wheezing as he tried to draw in a breath. "Lungs don't work like…"

"Dan, stop talking and let us help you. We'll go see Doc Parker." Alex put Dan's arm over his shoulder. The older man was taller than him by a few inches and he was still solid. He leaned heavily on Alex as they headed across the dusty yard to Alex's truck.

"I don't need the doc." Dan gave one last attempt. "Trouble. I knew when she knocked on my door that she'd be trouble."

Dan's granddaughter bristled at that. "Listen to me—"

"You old coot," Dan said, finishing her sentence, in a somewhat mocking tone.

"I wouldn't call you that." She opened the truck door. "We're taking you to the doctor, and like it or not, I'm not going anywhere."

"Dad-burn-it." Dan collapsed as they managed to maneuver him into the truck.

Alex gave her points for courage. She'd shown up on Dan's doorstep like a rain-soaked kitten tossed to the curb. Today the kitten had claws and she wasn't walking out on a grandfather who wasn't going to make her visit easy.

Alex had to admit, if he wasn't so tangled up in his bucking-bulls business, and in his past, a woman with her kind of spunk would be the woman to have in his life.

But he wasn't anything close to solvent and she wasn't the kind of woman who looked twice at a cowboy like him.

Chapter Three

The doctor's office was in an old convenience-store building on the south edge of Bluebonnet Springs. Alex drove them there in less than five minutes, with Marissa's grandfather arguing the entire time that he was fine and didn't need that "quack doctor." Alex had merely grinned during the rant. Marissa had tried to get Dan to calm down because his lips were turning blue from lack of oxygen.

They pulled up to the clinic, and Alex parked next to the front door. Thanks to a brief phone call, the physician waited outside for them. He had an oxygen tank on wheels, and as Dan argued, the doctor placed the tubing in his nose.

"Don't fight me, Dan Wilson," Doc Parker said, as they helped Marissa's grandfather out of the truck. "I told you to keep oxygen at your house. Now you're going to have to do what I say and maybe you'll live a few more years."

"Don't talk like that," Dan said, inhaling deeply. "You'll scare the kids."

Doc shot them a look, his eyes narrowed. "They're young but they can handle reality. Where did you get this pretty young lady?"

"I reckon that's my granddaughter. She showed up on my doorstep like a stray puppy and now I can't get rid of her."

Once they were inside, Doc got Dan to sit down.

"Did you feed her?" Doc asked, giving her a swift smile as he examined her grandfather. "If you feed them, they won't go back where they came from."

"I reckon I fed her a sandwich last night and she had a cup of coffee this morning. To repay me, she nearly killed my best rooster."

Doc laughed. "That rooster had it coming, Dan. He tried to flog me when I was out there checking on you last week."

The physician put a stethoscope to her grandfather's chest, telling him to breathe, then moved it to the next spot. Dan obeyed, but he shivered from time to time, and Marissa could hear the wheezing even without the stethoscope. A movement out of the corner of her eye caught her attention. Alex moved to stand behind her. Briefly his hand touched her shoulder.

The comfort took her by surprise. Brief as it was, it untangled the emotions of the past twenty-four hours and brought an unexpected tightness to her throat.

Doc sat back and gave her grandfather a long look. "Now listen to me, you old coot, I'm sending you to the hospital. I called the ambulance before you got here because I figured that cold you've had finally knocked you down."

"I don't need the hospital." Dan paused to take a breath. "And I've got animals to take care of."

"You've got neighbors who will help." Doc Parker looked at Marissa, his gray eyes kind. "Can you talk some sense into him?"

How did she talk sense into someone she'd just met? She looked at the gruff man who was her grandfather and she wished she'd had twenty-six years of knowing him. He was salty and rough but already she loved him.

"Granddad…" she began. He looked up, his eyes narrowing. She couldn't back down. Not when it was something this serious. "I'm not going anywhere. I'll stay and take care of the animals. You go to the hospital and get better."

"He's trying to send me off to a nursing home," her grandfather said quietly. "I'm not doing that."

"No, he's sending you to the hospital. And then you're going back to your own place to tend to that worthless rooster." Marissa put a hand on his arm. It seemed a natural gesture, but she was surprised by how easy it was to reach out to him.

"I'll help her keep an eye on things." Alex inserted himself into the conversation.

"Keep an eye on her, too. She doesn't know a thing about cows." Her grandfather paused again to breathe. The color was slowly seeping back into his cheeks. "Don't you kill that rooster while I'm in the hospital." And then he raised his gaze to Alex. "And no fox better get in the henhouse, either." He took another long breath of the oxygen.

Doc rolled his eyes. "Dan, I'm sending you in for some IV antibiotics and a few tests. That's all. You'll be home in a few days at the latest."

"You're sure?" Dan asked.

"Pretty close to sure. And the ambulance is pulling in. Alex and your granddaughter can follow unless they want to ride with me." Doc Parker helped her grandfather to his feet, then he gave Marissa his attention. "Do you need to call your family?"

It was a normal question, but this wasn't a normal situation. Before she could answer, her grandfather waved his hand and stopped her.

"No, she won't be calling family. She's my family. My *only* family."

Doc raised a questioning brow. "Is that so?"

Again, Dan answered. "It is if I say so."

"Dan, you have to let her answer." Doc glanced at her as he continued to examine his patient.

"Yes, I'm his family. But Granddad, I will tell my mother what is going on."

"Bah," he said, waving her away. As if she would go.

Suddenly, the paramedics entered. Alex stood with her as they readied her grandfather. Memories crashed in, and she closed her eyes against the pain that the images brought. It had been so long, but seeing her grandfather on that gurney, it seemed more like yesterday.

In an instant she was ten again. Her mom was screaming. There were police cars. And she was alone, standing on the sidewalk, unable to scream, unable to cry. That day had changed her life. Since then, she had felt alone.

The paramedics were moving. Her grandfather was cursing them. She tried to shake off the pain of the past. A hand briefly touched hers, giving a slight squeeze.

She wasn't alone.

"Are you all right?" Alex asked in a husky whisper.

She nodded, her attention glued to the scene

taking place in front of her. She was okay. But she wasn't. She was about to fall apart.

"Sit down," he ordered. He led her to a chair.

She sat, then lifted her gaze to meet his. He squatted in front of her, putting him at eye level.

"I'm fine," she insisted.

"I don't believe you. I know what it looks like when a woman is about to come unglued. But trust me, he's going to be okay. He's too ornery for anything else."

"I know. It isn't…" She swallowed and met his gaze again. "I'm fine. It was just a memory. But I'm okay."

"Do you want to talk about it?"

She managed a shaky laugh because he didn't look like a man who really wanted to talk. "No, not really. I should go. Maybe I can ride with the doctor."

He put a hand out and helped her to her feet. "I'm driving you."

"I'm sure you have other things to do. You aren't responsible for me."

"I know I'm not, but I found you. Finders keepers and all of that childish stuff. And besides, you don't want to ride with Doc Parker." He leaned close as he said it. "He's had so many speeding tickets, they're about to take his license."

"Thank you," she said, smiling at his warning. No matter how she felt at this moment, she wasn't alone.

Alex walked with Marissa to his truck. A breeze kicked up, blowing dust across the parking lot. In the distance the ambulance turned on its siren, and he could see the flash of blue lights on the horizon. The woman standing next to him shivered violently as if a cold arctic wind had just blown through her. He reached into his truck, grabbed his jacket off the seat and placed it around her shoulders.

He didn't think it was the breeze that had chilled her. He'd watched her in Doc's office. He'd seen the moment that past met present— her eyes had darkened and the color had drained from her cheeks. He recognized a person getting hit head-on by a painful memory. It had happened to him more than once.

There were days he could still hear his teenage self tell his father he wouldn't last five seconds on the bull he was straddling. His father had laughed and said, *From your lips to God's ears.*

Thirty seconds later his father was gone. His last words, a whispered, *You were right.*

He had his past. It appeared Marissa might have her own.

He wouldn't pry because he didn't let anyone

pry into his memories. He helped her in the truck and then he got in and started it up. She was still stoic, still dry-eyed.

"Did you charge your phone?" he asked as they pulled onto the road.

"I'll have to buy a charger." She averted her gaze and concentrated on the passing scenery.

There wasn't much to Bluebonnet Springs. Main Street with its few business, the feed store and his aunt Essie's café. On the edge of town there was a convenience store and a strip mall with a couple of businesses. The rest of the town was made up of a few churches and a couple of streets lined with houses that had been built a few decades ago. There was a new subdivision being built in the east end of town. That had caused quite a stir and given the lunch crowd at Essie's something to talk about for a good month.

A city utilities truck was parked on the side of the road.

"They're putting up the Christmas lights," he told her, because the silence was deafening and he didn't know what else to say.

"Christmas isn't my favorite holiday." She cleared her throat. "I didn't mean it like that. Christmas is difficult for my family."

"I'm sorry." He sped up as they left town. "It's a big deal here in Bluebonnet."

She gave him a questioning look.

"Christmas," he responded. "They love Christmas in this town. They have a big community service. There are four churches in the area and they all come together and each one has a play or music. The whole month of December the shops are open late each Friday. They serve cookies and hot cocoa."

"That does sound nice," she answered. "Maybe I'll be around for that. If not, I might come back. We typically don't do a lot at Christmastime."

He wanted to ask her about her family, maybe even wanted to know why her blue eyes clouded with emotion as she told him that bit of insight into her life. But he knew better than to dig into someone else's life. He knew from his own past that families all had their private stories. After his dad died, his entire family had avoided attending church. Specifically, they'd avoided the Church of the Redeemed, the church their father had pastored with an abusive hand.

Maria, the youngest Palermo, hadn't lived through much of Jesse Palermo's craziness, so she hadn't struggled with her faith. The oldest, Lucy, had found it a little more difficult. Alex had found his way to a church service after a bull-riding event. He believed that service probably changed his life and set him on a new course.

His twin brother, Marcus… That was a whole other set of problems.

The woman sitting next to him had shut down a little after the topic of Christmas so he wasn't going to push.

He usually had something to say, a joke to crack, anything to ease the tension. But he couldn't find that old ease, not with her. What could he say to a woman he didn't really know? All he knew was that she'd been jilted on her wedding day. She was Dan's granddaughter. And she didn't really care for Christmas and he didn't know why.

Somewhere out there she had people who did know her. She had people who would have the right words. And they had the right to say the words she needed to hear.

"Do you want to use my phone?" he offered in the silence of the truck. "To call family?"

"That would be good. Thank you."

He handed her his cell phone. And then he listened as she spoke to her mother, explaining where she was and how she'd come to be there. At the end of the conversation she told her mom she would keep her posted on her grandfather's condition.

She ended the call, then ran a shaky hand through her now short hair. The brown layers were chunky and framed her face, making her eyes large and luminous. He took the phone from her, their fingers touching in the process. Blue eyes met his and she smiled.

"Thank you."

"Anytime."

He reached to turn up the radio. The classic country station was playing George Jones. A typical song about heartache.

"So, you're a teacher?" Suddenly he felt the need to fill the silence. He shot her a quick look. "Good thing you aren't a beautician."

Her laughter was soft but genuine. She glanced in the mirror on the visor. "Not my best work. After this, I'll stick to teaching the alphabet."

He gave her another a quick look. Yeah, she looked like a teacher. The kind that wiped faces, hugged kids when they fell and made math seem fun. He'd had one or two teachers like her. The teachers who looked past the rough-and-tumble little boy and told him they thought he mattered.

Those teachers had inspired him. He'd managed to achieve a few goals thanks to their tutoring and encouragement.

Soon they were nearing Killeen and the hospital. Marissa appeared lost in her own thoughts and he doubted he wanted to go where she'd gone.

It didn't take a genius to realize he was knee-deep in this woman's life. For some reason he kept wading in deeper. For a guy who prided himself on keeping to his goals and priorities, that came as a surprise.

The last thing he wanted was the worry that he wouldn't be able to help her. He didn't like the feeling of letting someone down. Or, worse, the moment when someone looked him in the eyes and told him not to worry about it, he couldn't have done anything to help.

Chapter Four

"You don't need to sit at my bedside," her grandfather mumbled. Something about the growling words seemed half-hearted to Marissa. Or maybe it was wishful thinking on her part. Maybe she wanted him to need her. Or she wanted to try to make up to him whatever it was he'd lost when her grandmother left.

"I know I don't need to be here." She moved the chair closer to his bed. "I *want* to be here."

He shook his head. "Do-gooders, always trying to make up for what other people did wrong. Like Alex over there. He's trying to make up for that crook of a father he had. You're trying to make up for your grandmother walking out on me. What the two of you need to do is take yourselves off and live your own lives. Not together, mind you. That would be another mistake."

Heat climbed into Marissa's cheeks and she

avoided looking at the man standing near the wall. But he moved, forcing her gaze to shift toward him. He pushed away from the wall he'd been leaning against and approached her grandfather's bed.

"Dan, you're just being grouchy. And your granddaughter is the wrong person to take it out on," he said.

The last thing she needed was for him to defend her. She shot him a warning look that he disregarded with that cool, cowboy way he had. As if nothing ever got under this skin.

"I'm not taking it out on her." Her grandfather patted the hand she'd rested on the rail of the bed. "I'm giving some advice. Go on about your life. I don't know why any man would dump you. Maybe it's the grandfather in me talking, but I think any man in his right mind would want you. And don't be looking at her like that, Alex Palermo. We all know you're not in your right mind. Marissa, you need to go back home to your folks and to your life. I imagine there's some pieces you need to pick up. Things you need to deal with."

"I already told you I'm staying," she said softly, hoping he wouldn't disagree.

He opened his mouth to say something and coughed instead. The cough lingered, turning his face dark red as he fought to catch his breath.

When she offered a glass of water, he raised his hand and shook his head.

"I'm fine. Water's good for nothing but washing dishes. And making coffee. Get me some coffee and you'll be my favorite granddaughter."

"As far as I know, I'm your only granddaughter."

His hand over hers tightened and his gaze caught and held hers. "I know."

Those two words shook her. She saw in his eyes that he did know. She saw sympathy and sadness. She saw understanding. How did he know? But she couldn't ask. Not yet.

"What if that fiancé of yours comes to his senses?" her grandfather asked.

"I don't think I'd be willing to revisit that relationship."

"I'll get you a cup of coffee, Dan," Alex offered, and quietly slipped from the room.

Silence hung between them. Marissa tried to turn away but her grandfather kept his hand on hers.

"I know about your sister." He patted her hand. "I can't imagine how that hurt you. It hurt me and I didn't know her. But you were young. How old?"

"Ten."

"Yes, ten. Your grandmother sent me the newspaper clipping. She was heartbroken."

The information unsettled Marissa. "You talked to my grandmother?"

"Yes, we talked. No, it was more like yipping. We yipped at each other. Like the coyotes you hear at sunset. We never did get along. She was city and I was country. We were oil and water. The two don't mix. She wanted shopping malls. I wanted cattle. We bought the camper and planned to build a house later. At first she loved the idea. It was romantic, the two of us making our own way. And then along came your mom and it was crowded. To make matters worse, it upset her wealthy daddy that we were living like that."

"So she left you."

"Yes, she left. For good reasons, mind you. But after a while she called and apologized. She sent me letters. I mailed her checks. She decided I wasn't fit to be a father and I agreed. I understood horses and cattle but not little girls. I guess from the mess I made of my marriage, I didn't understand women any better. And that's why you should go on home. It was nice meeting you and I hope you'll stay in touch, but you belong in Dallas, not Bluebonnet."

"How do you know where I belong?" Even she didn't know where she belonged.

"That's what your grandmother said when

I told her she shouldn't marry a cowboy from Bluebonnet Springs. And I was right."

"You're not right about me."

Footsteps announced Alex's return. She stepped away from the bed, moving to the window to look out at the city landscape.

"Did I need to give you more time?" Alex asked as he handed the coffee to her grandfather. He pushed the button to raise the back of the bed so that Dan could sit up a little higher.

"You can take my granddaughter on back to my place. I think her folks should be able to find their way down here to pick her up."

Marissa picked up her purse. "Don't tell me what to do. I'm not that easy to get rid of. I'm going back to your place because someone has to feed the dog. And that stupid rooster."

"Don't be picking on my rooster," Dan grumbled.

"I won't. And I'm also not going anywhere."

Alex chuckled. "Dan, I wasn't sure if she was really your granddaughter until just now. She's definitely stubborn enough to be a Wilson. You may have met your match."

"Go away. I need my rest. Didn't you hear the doctor?"

"I heard him." Marissa leaned in to kiss her grandfather's scruffy cheek. "Don't worry about a thing. I'll take care of your animals."

He patted her shoulder. "That's what I'm worried about."

He smiled, a twinkle in his faded blue eyes. Eyes she realized were the same as hers. She'd always wondered where she got her blue eyes. And her stubborn streak. Now she knew. For the first time in a very long time she felt connected. He might not want her, but in her grandfather she'd found someone who might understand who she was and how she felt.

It was late afternoon when they pulled up to Dan's camper. Marissa felt a strange sense of coming home. It was a world away from her home. It was completely out of her comfort zone. And yet there was something about this place... the fields, the cattle, even the rooster.

It was change. Maybe that's what she'd needed.

"You're actually going to stay here alone?" Alex asked as he moved to get out of the truck.

"Of course I am. Why wouldn't I?"

Alex shrugged as he headed for the barn. She hurried to keep up.

"Maybe you didn't hear Dan, but I did. Your grandmother was a city girl who broke his heart." He shot her a look. "She told him she wanted this life with him but when it came down to it, she couldn't hack it."

"I'm his granddaughter, not his wife. And I want to be here to help him."

"Suit yourself."

"So you don't think I can do this, either, do you?"

He headed through the barn, stopping to give her a look before scooping grain into a bucket. "I make it a habit not to get involved."

"Then you should go. I'll feed and do whatever needs to be done here."

He headed out a side door, whistling shrilly. She heard an answering whinny and then hooves beating across the hard-packed earth.

"You'll do whatever needs to be done?" He grinned as he poured feed in a trough. "There's a couple of cows about to calve. Do you know what to do with a downed cow that's been laboring too long?"

"I can look it up on the internet."

He grabbed her by the wrist, his hand strong and warm, and they moved back a few steps as a couple of horses headed for the trough. The animals didn't seem to want to share. Ears were pinned back and one turned to kick at the other. Marissa didn't need to be told twice to get out of the way of those flying hooves.

"Should you feed them separately?" she asked.

"Nah, they'll get over it once they get to the business of eating. They've been fighting that way for years. That's what Dan gets for buying mules."

"They're horses, aren't they?"

He pointed to the heads of the big, golden red animals.

"Those are not the ears of a horse. Dan sold his horses when he stopped training and he bought mules. They're sure-footed and he uses them for trail rides and hunting. But I'm sure you can look that up on the internet," he teased, punctuating his words with a wink.

"Stop making fun of me. When I decide to do something, I do it. I'm staying and I'm going to help my grandfather."

"Calm down, I'm not making fun of you."

Of course he wasn't. But she'd gotten used to Aidan and his brand of teasing, which she now realized had been more. He'd smiled as he pointed out her shortcomings, then he'd told her he was teasing. Now she could look back on the last two years and a relationship that had been chipping away at her hard-earned self-confidence.

She briefly closed her eyes. When she opened them he had stepped a little closer. His expression, soft and concerned, eased the tension building inside her.

"I'm calm," she said.

"I admire that you want to help Dan, even if

you don't know a thing about ranching. But don't you have a job you need to get back to?"

A few days ago she would have said that she did have a job. She had an apartment, a job and even a fiancé, who would now have been her husband.

"I have a new job but I don't start until mid-January. I have plenty of time to stay and help my grandfather."

The job now seemed like another area of her life she'd given over to her parents. It was a job they'd wanted for her and approved of. And she'd agreed to the private school even though she'd wanted something else. She'd been looking at a small rural school when her father told her he'd gotten her an interview with a friend.

"Suit yourself." He headed for the barn with the empty bucket. "I have to get home and get my own chores taken care of. Tomorrow morning you'll need to move a round bale to the cattle. They'll eat about two of those fifty-pound bags of grain. And then you'll need to feed the chickens and gather eggs. Don't forget Bub."

The list of chores made her take a step back and reevaluate the plan. She quickly swallowed past the lump that lodged in her throat. She could do this. The other thing she could do was ignore the humorous glint in his dark eyes and the dimple in his left cheek.

He was the complete opposite of Aidan. He was the opposite of what she knew about life and men. He laughed too easily and smiled too much. He was too carefree.

But her grandfather had commented on his life, making her think everything hadn't been so easy for Alex Palermo.

"I can do all of that," she informed him because he seemed to be waiting for confirmation.

"I think you probably can," he said, suddenly serious. "Don't forget to lock the doors tonight."

"Lock the doors. Of course."

The humor evaporated. "I'm serious. I know you want to stay here. And I know you can handle things, but these cattle rustlers are real and I don't want you to think you have to go out and tangle with them."

Her earlier ease with the situation dissolved with that warning. "What should I do if I see or hear something?"

"Call 911 and then call me. I'll write my number down for you. And let Bub sleep in the house with you. He looks like a drooling mess, but he's got a pretty vicious bark."

"Okay, I've got this."

He winked, then he kissed her cheek, taking

her completely by surprise. "Of course you do. I believe you can do this."

Alex heard a truck door slam. He walked out of the stall he'd been cleaning and spotted his sister Lucy getting out of her truck. She waved and headed his way. Lucy was proof that the Palermo family could overcome the past.

An abusive cult leader for a father. A mother who'd abandoned them. Some folks around town still gave them the stink eye, as if they were waiting for one of the Palermo kids to turn out like their father.

Years ago, Lucy had escaped, joining the army and then returning to start a protection business with her former army buddies. Last spring she'd finally come home to Bluebonnet and ended up marrying their neighbor, Dane Scott. And Lucy had adopted Maria's baby girl, Jewel.

The only problem with all of this was that Lucy suddenly was into everyone's business and thought all her siblings needed to be fixed. She'd turned into a mother.

"How's Dan doing?" she asked as she entered the barn.

Alex put the pitchfork back in the storage room. He closed the door of that room. Long ago it was the room their father had locked Lucy in when he'd learned of her teen relationship with Dane.

"He's good. Word travels fast in a small town."

"Yeah, it does. I was at Essie's." The café their aunt owned. "She said Doc came in after he'd gotten back from Killeen."

He knew that hopeful look in Lucy's eyes, she was thinking maybe there was something between him and Dan's granddaughter. He headed out the front door of the stable. The sun was setting and the air had cooled ten degrees with a wind coming out of the north. He figured there'd be frost on the ground when he woke up in the morning.

"I guess Dan's granddaughter is sticking around?" Lucy asked as she walked next to him.

"Is there a point to this visit?" He opened the door to the garage he'd had built since he returned home last spring. Inside were a couple of tractors and a farm truck. The equipment belonged to neighbors. The tools belonged to him.

"How's business?"

He pushed a rolling toolbox in the direction of the John Deere tractor. "Business is good. And I'm not interested in Dan's granddaughter, not as anything more than a neighbor in need. I'll remind you that it wasn't too long ago that you weren't interested in dating. Just because you've gone to the other side doesn't mean I'm going to."

Lucy sat on a rolling stool and watched him. Studied him, more like. The way a scientist studied an insect. "One of these days there will be a woman who makes you forget. Or at least helps you let go of the past."

"It isn't going to be this woman." By the past Lucy meant the women who couldn't be seen with him because their daddies didn't want them dating a Palermo. As a teenager it had hurt. As an adult, he guessed he didn't blame them.

His dad had been a cult leader who abused his family. And most people would have said the apple didn't fall far from the tree. For a long time he'd almost believed it, thinking that he had no choice but to grow up in the shadow of Jesse Palermo.

He slid under the tractor and ignored his sister. Time was limited and Jerry Masters expected his tractor fixed in the next week. "I'm looking at buying some used equipment to sell."

"Can you do that and get those bulls ready to buck?"

"I can. Marcus is going to come home and help with the bulls. It works for us both. I invested my earnings. He blew through his like water." He scooted out and picked a different tool. Lucy was watching him, her dark eyes serious. "Stop worrying, Luce. I've got this."

"I always worry. It's my job."

"You don't have to worry."

"Yes, I do. I worry that Marcus is going to hurt himself or someone else. I worry that Maria has been talking to Jaxson Williams. And I worry that you still think it was all your fault. Everything."

"It was." He scooted back under the tractor, hoping she'd take the hint and leave. He knew better, but it was worth a try.

"You were a teenager and not responsible for our father's actions. Ever."

He gave up on the tractor, slid out and sat up, knees bent and arms resting on them. He gave his sister a long look. "Are you finished?"

The look in her eyes told him she wasn't. "No. I have a lot to say. You didn't lock me in that room. Our father did. You couldn't have busted me out. He wouldn't have allowed it. You didn't kill him. He made a choice to get on a bull that was rank and couldn't be ridden."

"I'm pretty sure I wished him a less-than-heavenly reward."

"You've regretted those words a thousand times."

"Are we done?" Because she hadn't yet brought up his best friend, Daniel, who had died under a bull. It had been Alex's job as a bull-fighter to protect him but he hadn't. He had a long history of not being able to protect the people he cared about.

Lucy shook her head and he knew the worst was yet to come.

"What is it?" he asked when she didn't spit it out.

"Mom."

Great. This was going downhill fast. Deloris Palermo had a habit of putting her kids last. She'd skated in and out of their lives for the last dozen years.

Lucy sighed. "She took out a mortgage on the farm."

It took him a minute to make sense of those words.

"And?"

"And she hasn't been making the payments."

He wanted to punch something. Instead he sat there with a wrench in his hand, waiting, hoping she'd tell him it was all good somehow.

"Please give me some good news."

Lucy shook her head. "I'd love to but there isn't any. She hasn't made the payments in six months. I wouldn't have known if I hadn't seen a man at the end of the drive taking pictures. The place is going to be auctioned off."

"What do we do? I've invested most of my

savings in this business and the bulls. I know Marcus doesn't have two dimes to rub together."

"I don't know if you're right about Marcus. He's been winning lately. Mom said she'll sell her half to us if we want. She's being generous, she says. Because she won't make us buy the whole ranch. She said Dad wanted her to have half and the rest split between his four kids. So in order to get her name off the land we have to pay her half the appraised value."

"The appraised value of five hundred acres and a house." He hung his head, wishing he could start this day over. "If we do that, she has to pay the second mortgage. That or we pay her, less the amount she owes. But do you really want to go in on this? Now that you're married, it doesn't seem like this should be your problem."

"We stick together, Alex. All of our lives we've only had each other. That doesn't change just because I'm married."

He tossed the wrench to the ground and did something he rarely did: he gave his sister a quick hug. "Thanks."

She hugged him back, the gesture awkward. "You're welcome."

He headed back to his tools. "So now I just have to figure out how to scrounge up a down payment. And face the reality that our own mother has put us in debt."

"Yeah."

"And you ask me why I'm not interested in a relationship. From what I can see, people who say they care tend to just rip each other to pieces."

"There's a difference between people who care and people who *say* they care. You've never let me down. I don't know if I've ever said it, but I love you, Alex."

He blinked to clear his blurry vision. Because he wouldn't let her make him cry. "I have to get up early," he said as he wiped his hands on a towel. "And you have kids to take care of and a husband probably wondering where you are."

"I'm sorry. I shouldn't have brought this up."

He managed a grin. "Remember when you used to stay out of our business and just let us all live our lives?"

"I seem to remember that person. I was a little bit broken, too."

"I'm not broken. I'm not even fragile. I'm cautious."

"And you're not *cautiously* interested in Dan's granddaughter?" she asked as she stood at the door, preparing to leave.

"No. I'm not interested. I found her on the side of the road in her wedding dress. If that doesn't scream trouble, I don't know what does."

Lucy's eyes widened. "A wedding dress?

That's a part of the story no one is talking about. Including you."

He was filled with some kind of strange loyalty and protectiveness. Hadn't he just said he wasn't getting tangled up in Marissa Walker's life?

"It's a part of the story that doesn't need to be talked about. No one ought to be walking down a back road on their wedding day, in the dress and without the groom."

Lucy gave him a long look. "You're right. But when you said she needed extra clothes, you didn't mention the dress."

"I didn't think it was anyone's business but hers."

"It's a good thing you're the one who found her."

"I guess it is. I'll see you later, sis." He reached to open the door for her. With a quick hug, she left.

He watched her truck head down the drive and then he went back inside the garage. Focusing on the tractor helped him keep his mind busy and kept him from worrying too much about the mortgage and buying the ranch he'd always considered his home. Fixing that tractor also kept him from thinking about Marissa.

Kind of.

He didn't want to think about blue eyes that rivaled the bluebonnets his hometown was named for. Or the blue of the sky on a clear winter day. He didn't want to think about how she'd managed to pull herself together, even though she had to be pretty close to devastated.

He couldn't help but think she needed family. Or a friend. Someone to help her through what had to be a pretty difficult time.

Someone who was not him.

Chapter Five

The gray light of early dawn peeked through a crack in the curtains. Marissa tried to roll over on the lumpy sofa but a bigger lump kept her from moving. She pushed at the drooling dog that had climbed up and was stretched out next to her.

"Down, Bub."

The dog groaned, then made a noise that was followed by a foul smell. She pushed him off the sofa and sat up, holding a hand over her nose.

"You are the most disgusting animal."

Bub just looked at her with his soulful eyes, his skin sagging downward, ears slightly perked. His tail thumped the faded carpet. Then he got up and lumbered to the door.

She followed, pushing the door open to the cool air. The rooster was sitting on the porch rail. As if on cue, he bristled his feathers and starting crowing.

"Good morning to you, too." She closed the door, shutting out the rooster and the noxious dog.

Blurry-eyed from lack of sleep, she headed for the coffeepot. She found coffee in a canister and filters in the cabinet. The refrigerator, as she'd learned the previous evening, didn't contain much in the way of food. Her grandfather seemed to live on eggs, skim milk and bologna.

She didn't know how he ever got to sleep. The quiet country seemed so loud compared to the sounds of the city. All night long she could hear the wind whistling through windows, the creaking of the camper settling, an occasional coyote howling and cattle mooing in the distance.

She put eggs on to boil and sat down at the table with a pad and a pen. She needed a list. Her life was about lists. It was important to her that she stay organized and stay on schedule. As she put pen to paper, she placed a fishing magazine on the pad to keep her penmanship level.

Tricks of the trade, she told herself. Before being diagnosed with dyslexia she had learned to compensate for her disability on her own. She'd learned to block off sections of reading material and use rulers to make her writing stay on one line—she'd never understood how these difficult tasks seemed to come easy for everyone else.

As she wrote out a list that included feeding livestock, cleaning, picking up groceries and visiting her grandfather, her phone rang. Her mom. It was too early for a lecture. She let it go to voice mail.

A text came through a few minutes later.

You have responsibilities, a job and a family. When will you be home?

She stared at the text for a full minute. Then she got up to pour herself a cup of coffee. Why couldn't her mother say something comforting? Why couldn't she tell Marissa that it wasn't her fault? That yes, Aidan had hurt her, but she would get past this. There were so many things a mother could say to comfort a child. But her mother had ceased being that person when Lisa died. She'd burrowed into her own pain, forgetting the daughter who still lived. A girl who had lost a sister and been overcome with guilt.

What they never talked about, what no one ever said, was that it had been her fault. Because of her, they'd all lost the thing they treasured most—her sister. Her parents' first child. And they never talked about it. Ever.

She'd spent sixteen years trying to make it up

to her parents, always following the rules, always working twice as hard. She'd done whatever she could to make life easier for them, to cause less trouble.

Through it all, Marissa had felt guilty. Because she was alive and Lisa wasn't. She'd felt guilty each time she'd saw a glimpse of sadness in her parents' eyes or caught one of them looking at a picture of Lisa.

And every single day she'd missed the sister she should have grown up with.

Blinking back tears, she poured the coffee down the drain and turned off the burner under the eggs. She typed out a text to her mom, telling her she was sorry that she never seemed to be enough for them. But the words were too honest. Instead she deleted the message and texted her mom she was sorry and would come home soon. Maybe after Dan got out of the hospital. Without waiting for a reply, she walked out of the camper.

Cool air greeted her. She shoved her hands into the pockets of her jacket and walked a little faster.

Cattle mooed at her approach. Red, the rooster, hurried across the lawn, wings flapping. She grabbed a stick and turned to face her attacker. The rooster jumped at her, and when she shook the stick, he squawked as it brushed against him.

"Oh, come on, I didn't even hit you."

The rooster flew at her again, but when he saw the raised stick he changed course and settled on the ground, feathers ruffled and a lot of rooster indignation in evidence. As she continued to the barn he followed, still making agitated noises and ruffling his feathers as he marched along behind her. He didn't trust her. She wasn't feeling a lot of trust for him, either. Occasionally she shot a look back to make sure he kept his distance.

As she entered the barn, a phone rang. She followed the sound to the feed room. An old rotary phone hung from the wall. She picked it up and answered.

The caller stuttered at her hello, and when Marissa asked who was calling, there was a long pause.

"This is Sheila from the IRS calling to speak to Mr. Wilson," the woman said, her tone hesitant.

"I'm sorry, he isn't here. Can I help you?"

"No, you can't. It's a matter of some importance. Could you please give him a message that I called?"

"I'll tell him." She hung up, staring at the avocado-green phone that hung on the rough wood-plank wall.

She wasn't about to give her grandfather that

message while he was hospitalized. But maybe the call explained the cattle that Alex had insisted were missing and had been sold off, and the run-down conditions of the property. How much could Dan possibly owe?

She stood there in the quiet, musty barn and replayed the call in her mind. Did the IRS actually make phone calls asking for money? A cat mewed. She glanced around and saw it sitting on the door that led to an empty stall. It licked a paw and surveyed her, then turned its attention to the rooster.

"Do you get fed, too?" she asked the cat. It looked at her with amber-colored eyes.

Inside the feed room she searched cabinets and buckets until she found a bag of cat food. She poured some in a metal dish she found in the aisle of the barn.

Marissa returned to the feed room, where she poured a few cans of grain into a bucket, the way Alex had done when he'd fed the mules the previous day.

Outside the air was still cool and a trace of frost remained on the grass. She had found leather work gloves in the feed room. They were loose on her hands but at least offered some warmth. The mules grazed a short distance away. When they spotted her pouring feed in the metal trough their heads went up. They watched curiously for a moment before heading her way. She emptied the bucket and then moved away. Having witnessed those hooves yesterday she had no desire to be too close.

She leaned against the side of the barn, breathing in the cool air. In the distance a bird swooped low over the field. She watched as the hawk grabbed at something, then ascended, carrying its prey as it flew away.

Closing her eyes, she thought about her childhood and the Sunday morning services they had attended. It had been different then, when there had been four of them and they'd been happy. After Lisa's death it all changed. They didn't attend church. Holidays became quiet affairs with dinners at restaurants and limited decorations. The mourning should have faded and life should have returned to their home. She knew that now. As an adult she knew that something had been very broken in their home.

As a child she hadn't comprehended, she'd only guessed that she was to blame. Maybe if they had healed, maybe if things had returned to normal, she wouldn't have been attracted to Aidan, to his laughter and to his promises. She'd seen him as an escape.

A horse whinnied. She opened her eyes and surveyed the horizon until she spotted horse and rider coming across the field. The rider wore his hat low over his eyes, but even on their short acquaintance, she recognized Alex. He rode the horse with the same easy confidence that seemed to be his trademark.

But now that easy confidence got under her skin. She'd never possessed that personality trait. Instead she'd fought hard to feel somewhat accomplished. She'd had tutors in college, studied on her computer when possible and occasionally she'd paid someone to read assignments out loud for her so that she could process them easier. She was an auditory learner. Reading too much, trying to decipher words that jumped around the page, sometimes brought on a migraine.

She went inside the barn, avoiding him, avoiding the strange need to talk to him. That urge to talk to him got under her skin as much as his brazen confidence on the back of that horse.

Of course she couldn't escape him. He came in through the front double doors of the barn, leading the big gray horse behind him. The animal snorted and shook its head. Alex patted the horse's neck and spoke in a soothing voice, as if the horse was a small child in need of calming.

"He doesn't like new places," Alex explained as he approached. The horse, as if to prove him right, sidestepped like it had been spooked at something. Alex held tight to the reins, drawing the animal back to his side with a firm hand.

"I see. What are you doing here so early?"

He glanced at his watch. "Is it early?"

"You know it is."

He shrugged it off. "I've been up for a while. I thought I'd check and see how your night went."

"Good."

"You look tired." He stepped closer, bringing the horse with him. With his free hand he brushed at her cheek. "And you have something right there."

"You shouldn't point out that a woman looks tired." She paused, then went on, "I'm not sure why people talk about how quiet it is in the country. It's loud. Coyotes. Cattle. Wind."

"Those sounds are like a lullaby, you just have to get used to them."

"I won't be here long enough."

He led his horse to a stall, removed the saddle and bridle and then gave the animal a flake of hay from the nearby stack of square bales. Marissa watched, waiting for him to say something, anything. The silence was getting to her. This was what came from watching the old programs picked up on the broadcast antenna and then switching to her grandfather's hunting magazines.

With the horse happily munching on hay, Alex stepped out and latched the stall door. The cat prowled past him. Alex watched it for a few seconds, then looked up, grinning at Marissa.

"I'm assuming you won't be here for much longer, but Sunday after this one we're having a community dinner at church for anyone who wants to join us, and for the families who live in the shelter. My sister wanted to make sure I invited you and Dan to join us."

"There's a shelter in Bluebonnet?"

"For abused women trying to start new lives. Several have children."

"I'll talk to my grandfather. If we come, what should I bring?"

"I'm not sure. If you'd like to help me bake pies, you're more than welcome."

"You bake pies?"

"Best pies in the state. And no, I won't give you my recipe. But I will let you slice the apples."

"I don't know how I could refuse such an offer. But I'm sure I'll be gone by then." Because this wasn't her life. It was a distraction. This was the adult version of a child running away, but only making it to the end of the driveway with a favorite doll and a pillow.

This wasn't her life. This dusty barn with the rooster eating cat food, a horse munching on hay and a cowboy offering to let her help make apple pie. None of it was hers.

What did she have left? Not even the ring on her finger was legit. She hadn't thought about the ring. Not until she looked down and saw the glimmering gold and the sparkling diamond. She yanked it off her finger and contemplated throwing it.

"Don't," Alex said quietly, the way he'd spoken to the jittery horse.

She held it tightly in her hand. The ring was one more thing she'd have to deal with when she got home. She'd return it the same way she would return the flatware, the china and the blender.

"Marissa?"

She shook her head to ward off any questions that might undo the fragile hold she had on her emotions.

Before she could stop him he'd closed the distance between them and wrapped strong arms around her. He held her against him.

"It's wrong, what they say about not crying over spilled milk." He whispered the words against her temple. "If it's your milk and you wanted the milk, you should be able to cry about it."

"I don't want to cry," she insisted.

Unfortunately the tears did come. Standing there in the circle of his arms, she couldn't stop them from rolling down her cheeks. What she couldn't tell him was that she cried more for the loss of her family than she did for the man who had walked out on her.

Alex hadn't meant to hold her. It had just happened. She'd looked at him with those sky blue eyes and he hadn't been able to stop himself from stepping forward and pulling her close. After a few minutes, she pulled free and backed away from him. With a hand that trembled, she brushed away the tears.

"I'm sorry," he said. He took off his hat and swiped a hand through his hair, wishing he could think of something better to say.

"No, I'm sorry." She pointed to his shirt. "I might have soaked your shoulder."

With her tears.

He felt his mouth kick up because she made it easy to smile. "No problem, it'll dry. I usually waterproof my shirts when I'm planning to bring a woman to tears."

"You didn't," she said, then sighed. "It was a long night. I haven't had a lot of sleep."

"All that silence," he teased.

Her eyes flashed with relieved humor. "Yes, it was loud."

"I thought I'd help you feed. I know you have the internet to look up how to do it, but it might be quicker if I start the tractor and hook a bale for you."

"It might be. Especially since I don't know what you're talking about." She pulled on the gloves she'd probably found in a drawer somewhere. They were leather and too big for those tiny hands of hers.

He nodded his head toward the side door of the barn. "The tractor is this way."

They were outside in the cool air when she spoke again. "My grandfather got a call this morning. From the IRS."

He grabbed the handle and climbed the two steps to the door of the tractor. "They called this morning?"

She stood a few feet below him, looking up, the sun kissing her face. Looking at her, he kind of wished he wasn't the son of Jesse Palermo, and that he wasn't still scraping and clawing to earn respect. He wished he hadn't learned that he was going to have to go waist-deep into debt to keep his ranch.

And she had her own baggage, which included a rain-soaked wedding dress and the ring she'd slipped into her pocket not fifteen minutes earlier.

He'd had a lifetime of living with people's suspicious looks. Kids he'd gone to school with had been warned not to hang out with the Palermo kids. He'd learned a lot of hard lessons in his life, but the hardest had been about women. They liked bad boys. They liked the boys their fathers told them to stay away from. But they didn't marry those boys.

Not that he planned on getting married. This woman was the type that might look twice at a cowboy like him, but she sure wouldn't take him home to meet her parents.

"Alex?" Her voice brought him back to the present.

"Right, the IRS." Something wasn't adding up. The IRS and stolen cattle.

"Yeah, they called this morning. I'm worried it wasn't legit."

"I'm not sure, but I do know that Dan wouldn't want you involved. He's pretty private."

"He's my grandfather."

"Yeah, he is. But this is his private business."

"I'm still going to ask him."

"I thought you might. Do you want to climb up here and I'll help you get a bale of hay?" He reached down and she took his hand, allowing him to pull her up. The cab of the tractor wasn't meant for two but he squeezed her in next to him.

She smelled of spring flowers and soap. It was a sweet combination.

"What do we do?" she asked. "I mean, about the hay, not the IRS."

"We spike a bale and move it to the field for the cattle. I noticed the mules are grazing the grass down to the dirt. I'll get them a bale, too, so you don't have to worry about handling the square bales."

"Where is the hay?"

"Dan bought a truckload in the fall. The bales are against the fence row," he told her as he started the tractor. "Hands on the wheel. I'll handle the gears this time and you watch what I do so you can do it next time."

He bit back a grin as she took the wheel in her hands and focused.

"By myself?" She said it softly.

"Of course. If you're going to take care of things for Dan, you have to know how to drive the tractor."

She worried her bottom lip but she nodded. "Of course."

The tractor jumped as she hit the accelerator. To compensate she hit the brake. It reminded him of teaching his little sister to drive. Alex steadied himself and swallowed a chuckle when she shot him a questioning look. He raised a hand and nodded, indicating she should keep driving. She hit the accelerator again, this time a little more smoothly, and he relaxed.

When it came to backing the tractor in the direction of a bale of hay, he had to call it quits. He didn't think he or the tractor could take much more.

"I thought I was doing great," she said with amusement glimmering in those blue eyes of hers.

"Oh, you were amazing, but I'd feel like a slacker if I didn't do something."

"I doubt you're ever a slacker."

He chuckled. "And now she compliments me."

"I mean it."

"You don't know me well enough. I promise, I'm very good at messing up."

He wished he'd said anything but that because she got that look in her eyes. She wasn't the first or last woman that would look at him as a project, a man in need of a woman's soft touch.

She was the first to make him believe she might actually stand a chance. She didn't look strong enough to stand up against a stiff breeze. And yet, he almost believed she could stand up against his past. He always wondered what that woman would be like, the one he thought would be able to handle it.

He got his wayward thoughts back on track because it wasn't real. She had enough on her plate without hearing about his life or the baggage he'd been dragging around for most of his twenty-seven years.

"Let's get this hay to the cattle and I'll take you to town for breakfast."

There went common sense and logic. Out the window.

Fortunately she shook her head. "I need to go see my grandfather."

"How are you getting there?"

"I'm driving his truck. The keys were hanging by the door."

He dropped the bale and for a minute he didn't comment on the idea of her driving Dan's farm truck to Killeen. He positioned the spikes and got the bale rolling. Behind them the cattle were moving in on the hay he'd spread across the ground.

She watched, clearly thinking farmwork was a lot of fun and not the hard work it really was. He knew her kind. She'd enjoy it for a few days, then head on back to Dallas.

"You can't drive the truck," he told her as he headed the tractor back to the equipment barn. The three-sided building had an open front. Dan parked his baler, the tractor and the ATV inside. There was also an old tractor he'd retired but couldn't part with. The tractor had rolled with Dan on it once, about fifteen years ago. Still, he held on to the rusted-out piece of junk.

"Why can't I drive the truck?"

"Because it doesn't have tags. And I doubt you know how to drive a stick shift. Those are two pretty good reasons."

"His truck doesn't have tags?"

"Nope. It's a farm truck. Not that it's legal for him to drive it that way, but everyone kind of turns the other way when they see Dan driving through town. He doesn't leave Bluebonnet Springs and he does have insurance. But you can't drive it."

"Can I drive it to town to get groceries?"

Hadn't he just told her she couldn't? He shook his head.

"I can drive you to the store or the hospital."

He helped her down from the tractor, her small hand in his. He let go as soon as her feet hit the ground because her hand in his made him want to hold on a little longer.

But he didn't have time for chauffeuring her all over the state.

"You don't have to do that," she told him, letting him off the hook.

He repositioned his hat on his head as he studied her determined face. "Suit yourself. If you run into trouble, give me a call."

Then he left, telling himself he should feel as if he dodged a bullet. Instead he felt more like he'd just left a defenseless kitten on the side of the road. He wanted to go back, but he couldn't. He guessed he'd have to look at her the way he would look at that kitten. If he didn't help her, someone else would.

Chapter Six

It took Marissa a whole day to work up the courage to drive the truck. After she'd fed the livestock the next morning she grabbed the keys and headed out the door, glad that Alex hadn't shown up and wouldn't see her poor attempts at driving a stick shift. The last thing she wanted him to know was that she had watched a video showing her how to drive a stick-shift car.

Bub the bloodhound followed her across the yard to the truck. He plopped down under a tree, a big rawhide chew bone held beneath his paws. She thought he might be as skeptical as Alex. He chewed on the bone but occasionally he'd lift his head and watch her.

She could do this. She'd show them all. She shoved the key in the ignition and turned. The truck jumped forward and died. Bub picked up his bone and moved a safe distance away.

Aggravated, she ran through the instructions from the video she'd watched. The clutch. She'd forgotten to use the clutch. She tried again. This time she got the thing started, eased off the clutch and moved forward about twenty feet. The truck shuddered to a halt and died.

It took ten minutes for her to figure out the nuances of the gearshift, the clutch, the gas and brake. It took another five minutes to make it down the driveway to the road. Hunger gnawed at her stomach, pushing her to keep trying. She also didn't like to give up. One way or another she would learn to drive this truck.

She was tenacious. That's what her grandmother had told her. And from her grandmother, it had been a compliment. She'd told Marissa it took a strong woman to overcome difficult situations and survive in this world.

She wondered why her grandmother hadn't been more tenacious in her relationship with Dan Wilson.

Once she got to the main road she sort of had the hang of things. There were a few jerky starts, but she got the truck headed in the right direction. She also found that it wasn't so easy to drive. It constantly pulled toward the left and she had to fight to keep it in the lane.

When she reached the Bluebonnet city limits she took a deep breath and let her shoulders relax. She'd made it. She had driven the old truck all the way to town.

A siren split the air and she jerked her attention to the rearview mirror. The police car behind her definitely wasn't there to give her a friendly escort. She pulled over to the shoulder, the truck shaking at her quick maneuvering and downshifting. It spluttered to a stop and she sat there, hands on the wheel, breathing past the tightness in her chest. She glanced in the mirror again.

The officer got out of his car, his hand on his sidearm. As if dangerous criminals drove old farm trucks. He glanced at the back of the truck and then at her. She closed her eyes briefly and opened them to smile at the officer when he walked up to the window.

"Driver's license and registration. And could you tell me what you're doing in Dan Wilson's truck?"

"I'm his granddaughter, Marissa Walker." She reached for her purse.

"Slow and easy, keep your hands where I can see them."

Yes, she would keep her shaking hands where the officer, named Jones, could see them. "Dan is in the hospital. I needed to pick up groceries."

"I know where Dan is. I also know he's had some cattle disappear. So why don't you go ahead and show me your license and we'll figure this out."

A truck drove past. A familiar dark red truck.

"Great," she muttered to herself.

"Problem?" Officer Jones asked. He momentarily shifted his attention to the truck that slowed as it moved to the shoulder of the road just in front of them.

"No."

Other than being pulled over. Humiliated. Jilted. She could go on, but he didn't want the list. He didn't want to know that it had been a horrible few days. He didn't care that until he'd pulled her over, she'd actually been feeling very proud of herself because she was not only surviving, but she'd also managed to drive the stupid truck.

Although she tried to fight the urge to glance at the truck on the shoulder just fifty or so feet ahead of her, she couldn't help but look. Alex was just getting out. He adjusted his black cowboy hat, shook his head and started their way. Officer Jones let out an exasperated sigh.

"I'm going to have to call this in," he told her. "Take the keys out of the ignition and hand them to me. And don't get out of the truck."

"I'm not going to drive off."

The officer looked skeptical and held out his hand for the key.

"Tim, is there a problem?" Alex asked as he finally reached them.

"I know Dan is in the hospital, so I was surprised to see his truck heading down the road. I'm checking it out now."

"This is his granddaughter. If you'll let her go, I'll make sure she gets it parked before she runs someone off the road."

"I'm right here and I resent that," she informed the too-confident cowboy. He leaned against the side of the truck, then shot her a grin and winked.

She resented that wink. That smile. As if he was there to get her out of trouble. She could get herself out of trouble. She also resented the way she suddenly felt better, as if his presence changed things for her.

He was the last thing she needed.

The police officer glanced at her driver's license and then he handed it back to her. "I'm not sure why you think I should take your word for this, Alex."

"I wouldn't lie to you, Tim." He said it casually. But she noticed the way his mouth tightened and his eyes lost their humor.

"No?" Officer Jones asked. This time neither man smiled.

"No." Alex moved away from his casual position against the side of the truck. "I help Dan at his place. I'm not the person who would take from an old man."

The officer handed her back the keys she'd given him. "Get it off the road. I've turned a blind eye to Dan driving back and forth to town, but I have to draw the line somewhere."

"Of course," she murmured. "I understand."

"We'll park at the café and I'll have it towed back to Dan's place." Alex stepped a little closer and she could see how tense he was.

"Good plan." Officer Jones nodded in her direction. "Give Dan my best."

"I can just drive back to my grandfather's place," Marissa offered after the policeman had walked away.

Alex leaned against the door, and she pretended not to notice that he smelled good. Not expensive-cologne good, but soap-and-country-air good.

"Can you get this thing started and follow me to Essie's?" he asked.

"Of course. I got it to town, didn't I?"

He laughed a little. "Yeah, you sure did. And got yourself pulled over. If you'd called me, I would have given you a ride to town."

"You have your own stuff to take care of. And I need to learn to drive this thing. I talked to my grandfather. They're going to send him home today and I'll need to be able to pick him up."

"Not in this truck you won't. Not only is it not licensed, but it wouldn't make it to Killeen."

"What about the old sedan behind the trailer?"

"No battery and I doubt it's in any better shape."

"I'll call a taxi," she insisted.

"Let's just get something to eat and we'll discuss this later."

Because she was hungry, she gave in. "I'll follow you."

"Good thinking."

She watched him walk away, then she started the old farm truck, pumping the gas when it tried to cut out on her. As Alex pulled back onto the road, she eased off the clutch and prayed the stupid thing wouldn't die. It didn't. She smiled as she turned down Main Street, victorious over the old Ford.

Essie's café was a tan, metal-sided building attached to the local farm-supply store. Farm trucks, sedans and SUVs alike were parked in front of the café. In a nearby parking lot cattle mooed from inside a livestock trailer hooked up to a truck.

Alex got out of the truck and motioned her to join him. She grabbed her purse and followed. As they headed for the diner she heard a rustling sound and turned just as a pig ran down the street, a small dog running along next to it.

"Please tell me that wasn't a pig?" She shook her head. "And a three-legged poodle?"

He chuckled as his hand went around her arm and he guided her toward the steps. "That was indeed a potbellied pig. And his buddy, Patch. They belong to Homer Wilkins. Homer can't seem to keep the two of them inside. Or they wear him down and he lets them out. No one is sure which and the city council has a heck of a time dealing with it."

She followed him inside the café and it seemed that all conversations ceased at their arrival. The silence lasted only seconds, then the steady hum of voices picked back up.

"Hey, Alex, have a seat and I'll be with you in a few," the dark-haired waitress called out as she rushed to a table with several plates. "Aunt Essie is in the kitchen. She's fixing the sprayer on the sink."

"Does she need help, Libby?" Alex asked the waitress. She was probably in her late twenties, with her long hair in a ponytail and an obvious baby bump.

"I don't think I'd go in there if I was you." Libby headed toward the table Alex had guided Marissa to. On her way she picked up a coffeepot. "You won't believe what Bea has done. She tried to make tea by taking off the sprayer and shoving tea bags in the faucet. She said it just made sense to her that if you turned on the hot water that would work. You could spray tea into glasses and never have to make a pot of tea again."

"She didn't really do that, did she?" Marissa blurted out before she could stop herself. "I'm sorry."

Libby grinned. "Oh, she did. Bea is a sweetie and she can cook just about anything, but she can get herself in trouble if you don't keep watch over her. You must be Dan's granddaughter! I bet he is just tickled pink to have you in town."

"I don't think *tickled* would be the word," Alex said. "And I think I'll take your advice and stay away from the kitchen."

The door to the kitchen pushed open and a middle-aged woman shuffled out. Tears were streaming down her rounded cheeks. She wore a bright, floral-patterned dress, brown shoes and blue socks. She brushed the tears away and yanked the hairnet off her head.

"I'm quitting because she's mean," she sobbed as she looked back at the kitchen door. "You're just angry because it didn't work."

"And that is Bea, the woman who should be cooking everyone's breakfast." Alex got up from the table. "I'm going to see if I can't put this fire out."

"Alex, your aunt is mean." Bea grabbed a napkin from a table. "And she doesn't like me anymore."

Alex took hold of the older woman's arm and led her to their table. She sat, giving Marissa a suspicious glare. "Is she your sweetheart?"

Alex turned a little red around the ears. "No. She's Dan Wilson's granddaughter."

"That don't mean she isn't your sweetheart. You can't account for taste. Have you seen that silly dog and that pig? What the good Lord joins together let no man put asunder. I think that's how God works. He puts together the most unlikely. If you get married, can I bake the cake?"

Alex groaned. "Bea, we aren't getting married. I'm taking Marissa to see her grandfather. I'm just being neighborly."

"Hmm. That isn't nice. Shame on you. My mama told me once about Mr. Carson being neighborly and I seen his car parked in front of Nora Jeffries's house..."

Marissa burst into laughter and that earned her a glare from Bea and a warning look from Alex. Before either could comment, the door to the kitchen opened again and this time an older woman with long, graying dark hair hanging in a single braid walked out. She didn't look at all pleased as she headed toward their table.

"Bea, I got the tea bags out of the faucet. Don't ever do that again. I know you have some very good ideas, but next time will you please tell me your good ideas so I can tell you if it will work."

Bea nodded. "Yes, Miss Essie, I'm sorry. Now I'll go cook. If you don't mean to fire me. And you can explain to Alex, because he is your nephew, that being neighborly is a sin. My mama said so."

As Bea left, Marissa felt heat crawl up her neck and her stomach chose that moment to growl loudly.

"I should go after her and correct her, but I'm just too tired." Essie smiled at Marissa. "Don't let her bother you. She's just Bea and we all love her and take what she says with a grain of salt."

"Of course," Marissa responded.

Essie's gaze slid to Marissa. "How long are you planning on staying in town?"

With her coffee cup midway to her mouth, Marissa paused. How long? She hadn't really thought it through. She'd left the wedding knowing that she had to go somewhere else and for some reason it had seemed like a good idea to come here, to see her grandfather. And the longer she stayed, the less she wanted to leave.

This town. These people. They might be exactly what she needed to get over the humiliation of her failed wedding.

She spied a Christmas tree in the window

of the café, and in the distance she thought she heard church bells. For the first time in a long time, she felt at peace.

Alex watched the expressions that flitted over Marissa's face. First she'd been embarrassed and then maybe a little bit cornered. Now she looked like a woman contemplating a life change. Not that he blamed her. He knew how it felt to come home and face people his family had hurt. He knew how it felt to be whispered about.

He guessed that's what she had to look forward to when she returned home. Fortunately she'd have an easier time getting lost in the crowd in Dallas. In a town the size of Bluebonnet, everyone knew everything about everybody.

"I'm just staying a week. Or maybe two," Marissa finally answered. "I want to make sure my grandfather is well enough to take care of himself."

"Dan's been taking care of himself as long as I can remember," Essie replied without censure. She turned her attention to Alex. "And you. Friday is the carnival fund-raiser for the children at the shelter. I think there are six little ones we'll be buying gifts for. And the rest of the money we raise will go in the shelter fund. You said you'd help."

"I will. I'm bringing the pony. We'll give rides

and also let the kids pet him." Alex glanced at the menu. "Could we order before Marissa passes out from hunger?"

His aunt laughed. "I heard her stomach rumbling. Yes, give Libby your order. I need to make some phone calls. I have about half a dozen people setting up craft booths for the festival. I need to return phone calls and arrange for Walt Smith and his friends to play music."

"I know you'll let me know what I need to do," Alex said as he poured sugar in his coffee.

"Yes, I will. And you can start by calling your twin brother and asking him to come home soon. I know he is having a good year and making a lot of money, but he hasn't been home for a long time."

"I can't control him." Alex hoped she would leave it alone. He didn't want to have uncomfortable family conversations in front of a woman who didn't need to know all of their secrets.

If she stayed in town and listened to gossip, she'd find out soon enough. She'd learn that his father had been nothing but a con man who bilked money from the good men and woman of Bluebonnet. Soon Marissa and the rest of the folks in town would also learn that if he couldn't find the money, the Palermo ranch would be auctioned on the county courthouse steps.

Essie patted his arm. "You can't fix it by worrying about it."

Alex nodded and hoped she'd let it go. Fortunately Libby appeared, order pad in hand. As his aunt departed, she sat down and propped her feet up on a chair he scooted close for her.

"When are you going to have that baby?" he asked.

"From the way I feel right now, could be any second." She reached for the glass of water Alex wouldn't drink. "I'm so glad you always let me give you a glass of water. You're my favorite Palermo."

"You know that isn't true."

She gave him a serious look and then turned her attention to Marissa. "He fixed our tractor and didn't charge us. No way could we have gotten our hay crop in last fall without his help."

Alex tugged at his collar. "Stop."

"But he doesn't like for people to know what a decent guy he is."

"Yeah, that's me. So, could I have biscuits, gravy and a couple of fried eggs?" Alex looked over at Marissa. "What would you like?"

"The same. And more stories about Alex."

"Stop," he ordered.

Libby got up and laughed as she walked away from the table. "I'll refill your coffee in a minute."

"The carnival and fund-raiser are to buy

Christmas presents for kids at the shelter and around the community. This time of year it seems there is more need. The community likes to make sure the children are taken care of at Christmas," Alex explained.

"That's wonderful. I'd like to be involved if I'm here. I love that Christmas is important to the people in town."

"You won't have plans of your own with your family?"

"No. Not since…" She stopped herself. "It isn't. There are just the three of us. Some years we visit my father's family and other years we go away on a vacation."

It sounded lonely but he didn't say that. "What did you start to say? Since what?"

She shook her head. "Nothing. We used to attend church on Christmas. Things were different when I was younger."

He was left wondering what she'd meant to say and why things had changed for her family. He knew he should leave it alone. Knowing her stories put him much more firmly into her life. And that was the last place either of them needed him to be.

They were almost finished eating when Marissa's phone rang. She glanced at the caller ID, silenced the ringer and finished her last bite of food. It rang again almost immediately.

"You should probably answer it," he offered.

"I'd rather not."

"Why is that?" he asked.

"Because I don't want to be lectured. I don't want to hear that I've let them down. I try very hard to always do what is expected and what makes them happy and I had no control..." She stopped talking. "I'm sorry, I didn't mean to do that."

He was sorry, too, because of the hurt he saw in her eyes. And because he couldn't find a way to distance himself.

"You don't have to apologize," he told her.

Her words had tumbled out as if she hadn't expected to say them and he got the feeling she'd never said them to another living soul. Not exactly a helpful realization for a guy who didn't want to get this involved.

"No," she answered with hesitation. "I guess I don't have to apologize. Not to you. But I do need to apologize to my parents. If you don't mind, I'll step outside and call them back."

"Go ahead. I'll pay the bill and be out there in a minute. If you want, we can take Dan's truck back to his place and then I'll drive you to the hospital to see him. I'll even drive Dan's truck back to the farm and you can drive mine if you want."

That offer elicited a smile from her. But still she shook her head.

"You have a life and I'm sure things you need to do."

He did. But he couldn't very well leave her on her own.

"Make your call and then we'll go see Dan."

Alex was pouring himself another cup of coffee when Duncan Matthews, the pastor of the Bluebonnet Community Church, arrived. Alex motioned him to his table.

It had taken a lot of years for Alex to trust anyone associated with ministry. He guessed a lot of people in the area felt that way after having been victims of Jesse Palermo's brand of religion. The Church of the Redeemed had been a cult with Jesse as the leader, controlling lives, controlling finances and abusing his family. Duncan Matthews had shown up in town a couple of years ago and he'd slowly but surely started the process of renovating the church and helping people heal.

"Is that Dan's granddaughter out there on the phone?" Pastor Matthews asked as Alex filled his coffee cup.

"Yeah, it is."

"She's crying."

Alex started to swear but an amused look from the pastor caused him to swallow the words. Instead he carried the coffeepot back to the warmer and returned to the table, where he sat down, stretching his legs in front of him as he nursed his third, or maybe fourth, cup of coffee.

He wasn't going to her rescue.

"You're not going to check on her?" Pastor Matthews asked.

"It's a private conversation." And none of his business. He didn't want it to be his business.

Libby approached, her hand supporting her back as she looked less than happy. She sat down and pulled a pen out from behind her ear. "Pastor?"

"Libby, you look like you might want to go home and put your feet up."

"I think you might be right."

Alex happened to glance toward the front of the café, and when he did, he saw Marissa at the corner of the building wiping at her cheeks.

"I have to go."

Pastor Matthews stirred creamer into his coffee. "I thought you might."

He let the comment slide. He'd known this woman less than a week and it seemed like a lot of people had let her down. He knew how that felt. And he didn't want to be another person who let her down.

It didn't make sense but there was no way would he say it out loud.

Chapter Seven

Wednesday afternoon, Alex drove the twenty miles to his bank. He stood on the sidewalk of the business he'd used since he'd been old enough to save money. He didn't usually take the time to think about what he'd wear or even what he'd say. He went in, deposited money, ordered checks—whatever needed to be done. Things were different today. There was a lot riding on this meeting.

A lot had changed since his conversation with Lucy. He'd found out that the ranch would be auctioned off if they didn't come up with some money soon. Lucy's husband, Dane, had offered to bail them out. Alex wasn't crazy about that idea. Dane hadn't gotten them into this mess, their mother had.

He stepped into the bank. The tellers, the same women he would see each time he came to the bank, waved greetings to him. He nodded and headed past them.

"Alex, come into my office." Blake Adams motioned him into the glass-walled office at the back of the small bank.

Alex followed, feeling less than comfortable with the situation. First, he knew how much money it would take to buy their half of the ranch. Second, he knew the amount their mother had borrowed and he couldn't get over how she'd blown through that much cash.

He sat down across from the middle-aged man, who always seemed genuinely interested in their lives. He'd probably lose that interest when he learned what was needed.

"So, tell me what's going on and how I can help."

Alex spilled the story, knowing it was no use holding back. Blake listened, took notes, nodded his head frequently and groaned as the details unfolded.

When Alex was done, the older man steepled his hands and leaned back in his chair. He drew in a long breath and exhaled.

"I hate this for you all," he began. "That doesn't mean we can't do something. But it's going to take cash on your part. I know you've invested in cattle, bucking bulls and your business. I'm not telling you to sell off any of that, but I am telling you to make some careful decisions. Also, make sure this is what your siblings want. Don't take on a big mortgage if you're going to be stuck doing this alone."

"And if we do nothing?"

They both knew the answer to that question. If he did nothing, the ranch would be gone.

"I don't like the idea of you having to buy your mother's half of the ranch, but if that's what it takes to get you out of this mess, then I would probably do the same."

Alex rubbed a hand over his face. Cash. Something he didn't have a lot of.

"I appreciate your advice, Blake." Alex stood and reached for the other man's hand.

"Alex, I'm here to help. I've watched you grow up a lot in the past ten years. You've done well for yourself, and you've thought about your future. I know you're going to make the right decision and get through this. Here's a loan packet. Fill this out. Get me the documents I've listed in there."

Alex took the envelope and left. It was a warm day and the sun beat down on him as he crossed the parking lot to his truck. A truck parked next to his looked familiar. He pushed his hat back to get a better look and then he shook his head.

"Marcus," he said as he walked up to the passenger-side door.

"Alex," Marcus whispered, his voice hoarse.

"How'd you know where to find me?"

"Lucy told me." He shook his head. "I can't believe Mom did this."

"I'm not sure why we're surprised."

"I don't think I want the ranch," Marcus said. "Or anything to do with it."

Alex shouldn't have been surprised. Marcus had been running since he turned eighteen. Even when he was in town he stayed with a friend on the opposite side of Bluebonnet Springs. But Alex hadn't thought Marcus would turn his back on them. Or on the ranch.

"I can't do this on my own."

"Lucy will help," Marcus whispered.

"It's our home."

"It's *your* home," Marcus countered.

Alex pulled off his hat and swiped his arm across his brow. "Where are you headed?"

"I'm on my way to Kansas. But if you want to go to Killeen, I'll buy you lunch."

"Sure, why not." He placed his hat back on his head. "I'm picking the restaurant."

One side of his twin's mouth kicked up. "Sure."

Alex headed for his truck. As glad as he was to see his twin, he couldn't help but feel like things were going from bad to worse.

On the drive to Killeen he had a talk with

himself and the good Lord. Because he had to believe that this would work out. He had to believe that God had a plan.

He decided to call his sister. It was new, this relationship where he turned to Lucy. He'd avoided her for a long time after that night his dad had locked her in the barn. He'd felt as if he let her down and he hadn't been able to look her in the eyes for a long, long time.

He put his phone on speaker and placed it on the console. "Marcus isn't interested in helping."

"I talked to him earlier. I told him to cowboy up and tell you to your face. Did he?"

"Yeah, he did."

"We'll do this, Alex. Don't let it get to you. You can't force Marcus to choose the path you're choosing."

"I know. I still kind of feel gut-stomped."

"I know. This whole thing has been a bit of a shock. We'll figure something out. I promise."

"Right. So I guess Mom isn't coming to Christmas dinner."

Lucy laughed a little at his poor attempt at a joke. "No. I guess she isn't. I saw Dan in town. I guess you busted him out of the hospital yesterday."

"Yeah, we did." No. He and Marissa weren't a *we*. Or a *they*. Yesterday Dan had told her she could stay a few more days.

And then she'd be gone. Back to Dallas. Back to her life. She would be a kindergarten teacher. She'd meet a subdivision kind of guy who drove a big sedan. Or maybe one of those electric cars that had to be plugged in.

"Alex?"

"Sorry. Just thinking." He cleared his throat. "I'll sell the bulls."

"What?"

"The bulls. I invested a lot in them, and I can use that money to pay off the second mortgage. That'll buy me time to get a loan to buy out our mother. I'm afraid if we don't, she'll do something else to get us further into debt."

"Calm down. Don't rush into anything."

"I guess we don't have time to sit on our hands." He approached a steak house. "I've got to go. Marcus is buying me lunch."

She hung up and he made the turn into the parking lot of the restaurant. His brain had taken a serious left turn and was stuck on Marissa. He'd never been the person who saw himself as part of a couple. He'd never relied on anyone other than his siblings.

That's why it didn't make sense that he didn't want to be at this restaurant with his twin. He wanted to be in Bluebonnet Springs sitting at the tiny table in Dan's camper, having a cup of coffee with Marissa. As much as he wanted to be with her, he had to be the last thing she needed or wanted in her life.

Marissa held tight to the kitten she'd found in the barn. It didn't really seem to want to be held. She deduced that from the way it was clawing and biting at her gloved hands. But she wouldn't let go. The other grown cat she'd seen stalking a mouse the previous day had cornered the kitten in the feed room and Marissa had been positive the cat meant to tear the kitten to pieces.

Using her teeth, she pulled the glove off her left hand and held the kitten tight with her right hand. She opened the door of the camper and stepped inside. Her grandfather looked up from his recliner, his eyes narrowing in on the gray kitten. He'd been home for a day, but already he was telling her to go on back to Dallas. She'd told him she needed to be here to help him. And besides, she was getting pretty good at driving a tractor and she finally knew the difference between a cow and a bull.

"No," he said as he pointed to the front door. "Barn cats stay in the barn."

He'd been acting what Alex called "cantankerous" since they brought him home. He'd complained about the wreath she'd put on the front door. He'd told her he wasn't going to let her put up any kind of Christmas tree. There wasn't room for one, he insisted. And he was probably right, but she couldn't imagine not having a tree. Even if she wasn't staying, she wanted him to have one.

"The old tomcat was after him," she explained. She took the kitten to the kitchen and poured it a small bowl of milk.

"I don't care if he was using that kitten to bait a mousetrap. It goes back to the barn."

She gave him a warning look. "You'll have yourself coughing if you don't stop."

"Bah." He waved a dismissive hand. "You'll have me coughing if you don't stop testing my patience."

"I'm not sure what you mean. I hadn't noticed you have any patience."

He pushed himself up out of the chair and headed for the kitchen, a frown firmly in place, but she'd seen the hint of a grin. "I don't. And that's why your grandmother left me. I was a drunk with a short fuse."

The revelation shocked her.

He poured himself a glass of juice. "And you remind me of her. You don't have any quit in you."

She smiled at the compliment. Even if he hadn't meant for it to be one. "I couldn't find that cow you told me to look for."

He set down his glass on the counter. "Well,

maybe you should have said that the minute you walked through the door instead of worrying about that kitten."

"I'm sorry. I'll go back out and look again. I just wanted to get a heavier coat."

"I'll go." He was already heading for the tiny closet by the front door.

"No, Granddad. You have to stay inside."

"I have to find that cow. You don't understand her value. And the value of her calf. I can't afford to leave them out there to die."

"Granddad, Alex said you have cattle disappearing. We noticed four-wheeler tracks. And the IRS called. I'm worried about you."

"It isn't any of your dad-burned business."

"It is my business. You're my grandfather."

He pointed a shaking finger at her. "You didn't seem to care about that until your groom walked out on you."

"I would have cared had I known. And stop trying to badger me. This is serious. We need to call the police."

"Don't you dare call the police. I'll take care of this. Once I get the IRS paid off, they'll go back to bothering other taxpayers."

Except she wasn't convinced it was the IRS. How did she tell him she thought he was being duped?

"I have to go get that cow." He pulled open the door of the tiny closet.

"I'll go get Alex," she said quickly, before he could head out the front door. As much as she didn't want to lean on their neighbor so much, he was really the only person she knew to go to for help.

"Alex has his own set of troubles." He gave her a pointed look. "And don't be thinking that's the direction you need to be turning. I know how you young people are. You get hurt and you immediately rebound to whoever you can find. Alex is the last person a girl like you needs to take up with."

"I'm not looking for a rebound relationship," she informed him as she watched the kitten lap up the milk. "I'm trying to help you, and Alex seems to have the same goal. And he's really the only person I know in town, so I thought I would go get him."

"Uh-huh," he said. "I know what it's like, you city gals and the lure of a cowboy. I wasn't always this old."

"I'm not interested in a cowboy. I'm not interested in anyone. A little under a week ago I thought I was getting married and he walked out on me. There is no instant rebound from that."

The expression on his face softened. He hung

his jacket back in the closet and returned to the juice he'd left on the counter.

"No, I reckon there isn't an easy rebound from that. And I'm sorry. Sorry as anything that you thought you had to come here to me and not to your parents, or whatever friends you have in Dallas. It doesn't seem natural that you'd want to be here with someone you've never met before."

"It seemed natural to me," she said.

Awkwardly he patted her arm. "I can't see how. Let me give you some advice anyway."

"Okay."

"Don't shut yourself off. Now, that doesn't mean I want to see you chasing after Alex Palermo. He isn't right for you. But I wouldn't want you to be anything like me. After your grandmother left, I decided there wasn't much about me that anyone else would want. Oh, I quit drinking, because I thought she might come back someday. But she didn't. And after some years went by I decided I was just meant to be alone. But being alone, it can be lonely."

Sage advice from a man who had lived with much regret. She stood on tiptoe to kiss his weathered cheek. "Thank you."

"Go on now. Don't thank me. I still don't want you here, underfoot and bringing barn cats in my house."

"Of course you don't. If you'll watch the kit-

ten, I'll see if I can get us some help to find your cow and calf."

"That would be good. I need to take a few head to auction next week." He picked up the kitten. "Take it back to the barn. Not enough room in here for Bub and a cat."

She took the kitten.

"I'll go get Alex."

She was heading for the door when he stopped her. "How'd you learn to drive that truck?"

"Looked it up on the internet," she answered. She left smiling, because she heard him chuckling and saying something about her backbone.

The bull in the chute bucked, kicking at the metal enclosure, and then rattled the gate with his horns. Alex grabbed the horns and brought the bull's head back around. The teenager standing on the catwalk backed up a bit, his eyes widening as he watched the animal try to come out of the chute.

"Second thoughts?" Alex asked.

"No, of course not."

Alex laughed. The other boys leaned against the arena wall and looked as if they were about to run for their mamas. They were neighbor kids who wanted to bull ride and their parents had given permission for them to buck bulls with Alex. His bulls needed the experience. The boys

needed experience and instruction. It was a win-win situation.

Unfortunately the boys also needed courage, which they hadn't gotten on steers that were used in the earlier stages of bull-riding training.

"Okay, I'm going to ride this bull and show you all how it's done. And then we'll try again on Hazardous Duty." As if he heard his name, the bull pushed against the metal of the pen.

He motioned the boys close. "Come on over and help me out. Jason, you get down there and be ready to open the gate. Dusty and Kyle, stand here with me and help me get settled."

The last thing he would admit to these boys was that he had no desire to get on the back of a bull. Not now. Not ever. Especially not in this arena. But if he was going to let these kids do it, he had to be willing to pull his rope on one of the rankest of the six bulls he owned.

For now. He didn't want to let go of this dream, to own bucking bulls. But every now and then he wondered why it was his dream.

He pushed his hat down tight and climbed over the side of the chute to settle on the back of the bull. The minute he got his seat, the bull started to shift and buck, trying to unseat him. He wished the eight seconds could start inside the gate because sometimes this was the tough-

est part, and could even be the most dangerous. He'd seen men broken and knocked out just trying to get their bull rope tied.

He pounded the resin-covered rope over his gloved hand. The bull went up but Dusty pushed him down and Kyle held Alex's shoulders. He heard a truck and he groaned. That sounded like Dan's truck. He hadn't seen Marissa since he helped her get Dan home the previous day. "Ready, Alex? He's just going to get more rowdy," Jason called from the dirt floor of the arena.

"Ready." He nodded once. The gate flew open.

He breathed past the first jolt and the left-hand turn he knew was coming. He blinked away the image of his father's prone figure on the arena floor. The bull bucked right twice and then he took a flying leap and belly rolled. As Alex flew through the air he caught a glimpse of a woman with short dark hair and heard her scream.

He hit the ground, rolled, covered his head with his arms and then felt the bull slam against him. White-hot pain slashed through his leg and his side. The bull came at him again.

He caught his breath and scrambled to get on his feet. Someone was there, distracting the bull. Jason. The kid grabbed at the bull and then ran for the gate. Dusty had the gate open for the bull.

Alex leaned forward, winded. When he straightened, Marissa was there. She looked small in Dan's straw hat and denim jacket.

He swiped at his face to clear his vision. "I lost my hat. And you should not be in this arena."

"Your hat? You're worried about losing a hat when you might have lost your life?" she yelled at him.

"I wouldn't lose my life." He took a cautious step forward and bit back a groan.

"Who would help me if you weren't here?"

He managed to chuckle. "People. There are plenty of people who can help you."

"I like you." She helped him walk out of the arena. "So I would be very offended if you got yourself killed by a bull."

He pulled free from her arms, and he admitted it took some doing. Not because he couldn't walk on his own, but because he liked being in her arms. They were slim but strong. They felt like a safe haven. He couldn't say that he'd ever felt that before.

And it frightened him more than being on the back of that bull. Because a safe haven was a place where a person took refuge. She couldn't be his. Ever.

But her words were ricocheting around in his brain. He could have been killed by that bull. She wasn't far off the mark.

"My dad died in that arena," he said softly, then moved ahead of her. She came after him. Though admittedly she didn't have to move too fast. He collapsed on the closest bench and put his head between his hands. She sat down next to him. Her shoulder brushed against his.

"I'm sorry," she whispered. She sat close to his side, her presence undoing something inside him. Something he'd kept boxed up and off-limits for years.

It might have been the hit to his head, but he was having a hard time understanding how she had managed, in such a short amount of time, to make him think things he'd never thought and feel things he'd never felt.

"Don't worry about," he replied.

"It has to be difficult, being here, knowing that you lost him here."

The truth happened to be pretty ugly and he didn't want to see the reaction on her face when he told her. But maybe if she knew the truth, she'd walk away from him and he wouldn't have to keep fighting his feelings for her every time they got close.

"I wanted him to die. I was a kid, just seventeen, and more than once I'd thought how much better life would be if he…"

"You were just a kid," she said, moving closer.

"Yes, a kid. And he was as mean as a snake. My sister has her own stories. We all do. But that's not why you're here."

"I'm sorry." Her hand settled on his cheek. He briefly closed his eyes and her hand slipped away.

"Childhood shouldn't be so difficult." She said it in a way that made him think she had experience with troubled childhoods. It made him want to ask questions of his own.

As if she knew what he was thinking, she walked away from him.

He swiped at his face and saw blood on his hand. He needed to clean himself up and get back to work. As he stood, he saw Marissa at the entrance to the arena talking to Jason, Dusty and Kyle. The three teenagers were listening intently, as if she was somehow in charge. He headed their way but they didn't wait. Jason did give him a salute as he turned and left.

"They're leaving but they put the bulls back in their pen first," Marissa said as she returned to his side.

"You don't have to stay, either."

"I think someone does have to stay. Plus, I can't go until you tell me what to do about a missing cow. Dan is beside himself and I'm afraid he'll try to go look for her." She moved his hand away to look at the cut on his head.

"It's fine."

"Of course it is."

"So you're here about one of Dan's cows?" he asked, trying to deflect her attention from him.

Her blue eyes flashed with humor. "Well, I certainly wasn't here to see you get knocked unconscious. It just worked out that way."

"Don't be dramatic. I was never unconscious," he argued as he pushed her hand away from the cut. "Ouch."

"Sorry. I don't think this is too deep. Do you have a first-aid kit?"

"In the tack room."

She glanced around. "And where would that be?"

"This way," he told her, not pulling away when she took his hand.

"You're limping."

"Yeah, he went after me pretty good."

"Do you need me to drive you to the ER? Or to Doc?"

He opened the door to the tack room. "I can doctor myself. A bandage on my head and maybe some ice on my knee and I'll be good to go."

"Where is the first-aid kit?" she asked.

"The cabinet. Maybe the second shelf."

"Okay, sit down and I'll get you fixed up." She maneuvered him to the seat in the corner of the room.

"We need to get that cow found," he told her.

"I'm sure she's fine." She wiped the wound clean and used a butterfly bandage. Her fingers were gentle, cool. He closed his eyes as she worked. Because if he looked into her eyes, he might lose himself.

"There." She finished. "What about your knee?"

He opened his eyes. "I'm good. I can walk it off."

"Really? You'll just walk it off?"

"Isn't that what you've been doing since I found you walking down the road?"

"Yes, I guess I have. And surprisingly, it doesn't hurt much."

"There you go. I'll walk it off and it won't hurt much." With a grimace he managed to stand. "But we should take care of that cow. Dan won't thank us if he's lost one of his good heifers."

"Will he be upset if I put up a Christmas tree, do you think?"

He took advantage of her nearness and slipped an arm around her waist. Just to steady himself, he told himself. And because she smelled good.

"I don't know if I remember Dan ever putting up a tree. But I don't think that's going to stop you."

"No, it won't." She allowed him to lean against her and he felt a little guilty. Not guilty enough to admit he didn't really need her help.

They left the barn walking side by side, her steps slow, in order to match his. When they got to the old farm truck, he leaned a little closer, tempted. He wanted to know what made this woman tick. What made her strong as steel and yet tender. She taught kindergarten. She cared about a grandfather she hadn't known until recently.

"I know I shouldn't. So let's just blame this on the head injury," he murmured low, close to her ear. He pulled off the straw hat she wore and pulled her closer, hoping she wouldn't back away.

Once upon a time he'd told Aunt Essie he would never get married because he would never fall in love. Essie had laughed and told him that the right woman would come along and no matter how hard he fought, he wouldn't be able to keep from loving her.

Marissa was everything he shouldn't want. And he was the last thing she needed.

He reminded himself of the mortgage on the ranch, hoping it would bring him back to his senses. He told himself this woman deserved better than he could ever give her. But then the breeze kicked up and blew soft tendrils of hair around her face and a tropical scent filled the air.

He moved close enough to feel her breath against his neck. And then he kissed her. His lips brushed hers. With that kiss, his whole world spun a little bit out of control. And he couldn't blame it on the blow to his head. Not really.

It took him by surprise, the way it felt to hold her, to kiss her. It took him by surprise because she kissed him back and her hands fluttered on his shoulders until they settled.

Then suddenly, it was over.

"No," she whispered, pulling away from him. "This isn't why I'm here. I'm not here to jump from a failed relationship to a relationship that can't be anything more than temporary."

"It was a kiss, not a proposal," he assured her with humor he was nowhere close to feeling. "Temporary is the only kind of relationship I've ever had."

"Yes, me, too." With that she got in the truck and cranked the engine to life. He stepped back, letting her go.

It was better that way. She'd hold on to that iron will of hers and he would learn to stay on his side of the fence. But then he remembered she had a cow to find, so he headed to his truck.

Out of the frying pan and into the fire.

Chapter Eight

❧

She shouldn't have kissed him. Marissa parked the truck and then rested her forehead on the steering wheel. What had she been thinking, kissing Alex? How stinking cute he was in his jeans and faded T-shirt. She'd thought about how he'd fallen off that bull and managed to walk away. And then his arms had been around her. And she'd wanted to know that a man found her attractive.

Fortunately she'd come to her senses. Or maybe unfortunately. Because she'd loved being in his arms. She'd loved the way he'd held her as if she was precious to him. But he liked temporary. He'd said it himself.

She didn't want to be anyone's temporary romance, ever again.

She leaned back in the seat and sat there for a minute in that old truck of her grandfather's.

It smelled of cattle, oil and age. The seat had a rip that he'd fixed with gray duct tape. Why was she here? Driving this old truck? Searching for cattle? Feeding barn cats?

Kissing cowboys.

This wasn't her life.

But she couldn't leave. Her grandfather wasn't healthy and he needed her help. If someone was taking advantage of him, she needed to figure it out. Headlights flashed through the cab of the truck. She knew who it would be. A moment later Alex was climbing in the passenger seat. He tossed her the hat he'd pulled off her head when he'd kissed her.

"Thought I should return this."

"Thank you." She shoved it back on her head.

"I'm sorry," he said.

She glanced at him and couldn't help but smile. He was cute. Even with his big ears. She thought about telling him, but why add to that ego of his.

"Please don't apologize," she said instead. "Just help me find that cow."

"That's the other reason that I'm here."

"I thought I heard her earlier. Maybe down by that pond. But it was getting dark and I knew if I found her, I wouldn't know what to do with her."

"Don't worry, we have everything we need in the back of the truck."

She started the truck and headed for the field. She noticed he didn't grimace too much at her driving.

"I'm getting better at this," she informed him.

"I agree. By the time you leave, you'll be an old hand on the farm. When you get back to the city you won't know how to drive your car anymore, or remember how to handle that city traffic."

"I sure don't miss that traffic."

"Oh, you will miss it." He said it with authority. "The same way I kind of like the city for a little while, but then I'm ready to get back here. No stoplights. No traffic jams."

She didn't argue with him, but what if she went back to the city and she wasn't happy there? What would she do then? Come back here to her grandfather's camper? And no job.

The conversation trailed off. Marissa drove around the pond, searching for any sign of the missing cow. Finally the headlights found her. She was on her side in a brushy area near the pond.

"There she is. Be sure to set the emergency brake. I wouldn't want Dan's truck to roll into the pond." Alex jumped out of the truck. Marissa did as he'd told her, then she followed him.

When the cow saw them, she let out a plaintive cry and made a strong attempt to push. Alex examined her and shook his head.

"I'm only seeing one hoof."

"Do we call a doctor?"

He laughed. "No, we don't call a vet. There are times when that's necessary but usually we can handle it ourselves. I'm going to see if I can get that other hoof and then we'll see if she can't do this on her own. If not, we'll pull the calf. There's a chain and pulley in the truck."

Chains? Pulleys? She cringed, thinking how difficult and painful this sounded.

Alex took over. It took some time but eventually the calf slid out. The mama was exhausted but she cleaned her baby, then managed to get to her feet.

Marissa watched, completely enthralled by the process. She'd never seen a birth. Not even kittens. Alex stepped to her side, wiping his hands on a rag he'd found in the back of the truck. Side by side they watched as the calf found his legs and stood, wobbly but healthy. The cow nudged him, her long tongue taking swipes down his back. Eventually he found his way to her belly and was able to get his first meal.

"Will they be okay now?" Marissa asked as they walked away.

"They'll be fine. She'll feed him and then she'll find the rest of the herd."

"But it's cold."

"She'll keep him warm," Alex reassured her. He opened the passenger door of the truck. "Climb in. I'm driving."

"I can drive."

"I'm driving because you behind the wheel of this truck is more frightening than eight seconds on the back of a bull and thirty seconds under its hooves."

"You said I was doing better."

He winked. "You are, but I'm just not sure I can handle the return trip right now."

"I made sloppy joes for dinner and I was going to invite you to join us. Now, maybe not."

"I take it back. Really. For sloppy joes, I'll even let you drive." He bumped his shoulder against hers.

A few minutes later they walked through the front door of the camper. Bub got off the couch to greet them, but before Marissa would pet him, she grabbed the towel she'd left on the coatrack. She wiped the drool from the dog's face and he thanked her with a soft woof.

Marissa's grandfather was on the phone. He held up a finger to keep them quiet. Marissa nodded and leaned to pull off her shoes. Next to her, Alex did the same.

Dan hung up, saying a few things he shouldn't have said.

"Who was that?" Marissa asked as she headed for the kitchen and the slow cooker she'd filled with sloppy-joe ingredients.

"That was the lady from the IRS. They think I owe them another payment."

"Dan, you have to let me look at your paperwork and anything they've sent you. Please."

He shook his head. "I've been taking care of myself for a good long time, young lady."

"There's nothing wrong with letting someone else help."

He switched off the television. "I know there isn't. But this is my business."

"Right. You're right." She stirred the hamburger and then turned off the cooker. "Are you hungry?"

"Of course I am. It's pretty near bedtime."

She glanced at the clock on the stove. "It's seven o'clock."

Alex had stepped to the sink and was washing his hands and arms. "Dan, you have a bull calf."

"You found the cow? I'm glad. She's one I wouldn't want to lose. They're both healthy?"

"They're both healthy," Alex assured him. "Dan, let her look at the papers."

"Since when do you get in my business, Alex?"

"I'm getting in your business because you're losing livestock and now you're paying out money you might not have to pay. Someone needs to figure this out. And you probably need to call the police."

"You should worry about your own affairs. The county paper came out and there's an interesting list of properties up for auction."

Alex didn't respond, he just shook his head. Her grandfather had gotten up and made it to the kitchen, stopping once to catch his breath. He had an oxygen tank nearby but she knew he wouldn't use it until he absolutely had to.

"The only reason you're getting in my business," Dan said to Alex as he poured himself a cup of tea, "is because I have a pretty granddaughter living here."

"And you're getting in my business because I'm a Palermo," Alex muttered.

"You said it, not me," her grandfather responded.

"Stop. Both of you," Marissa yelled. "Sit at the table and I'll get you a plate."

Her grandfather sat down. Alex helped her get the plates and food on the table. And then they all sat. The table was small, more of a miniature booth than a dining room table. When her grandfather wouldn't budge from his seat, she sat next to Alex. They fixed their plates, then Alex cleared his throat.

"What?" Dan grumbled.

"I'd like to ask for the blessing." Alex grinned at Dan.

"Suddenly he gets religious and makes a nuisance of himself." Dan bowed his head. "Make it quick, Palermo."

Marissa bowed her head. Her breath caught when Alex slipped his hand over hers. His fingers were warm and strong. His prayer was sweet. Her heart tripped over the moment, getting tangled up in something she knew could be dangerous.

Dangerous in a sweet, tempting way that made it hard to resist.

Alex lifted the fence-post driver and slammed it down on the metal post. It vibrated through his arm and his back, reminding him of the spill he'd taken from the bull the previous day. He raised it and brought it down on the post again.

Today he was repairing fences. But he was also taking his frustrations out on those posts. It was a good thing they needed some serious pounding to get them in the ground. He raised the driver one more time on the post and then he stepped back, pulling a handkerchief from his pocket to wipe his brow.

A truck pulled up the drive and parked by the fence. Pastor Matthews got out. He eyed the fence and the post driver, and started to get back in his truck. Through the windshield Alex could see his grin.

"Oh, no, you're already here." Alex motioned him out of the truck. "Showing up is the same as volunteering. Wasn't that the sermon a few weeks ago?"

Pastor Matthews adjusted his ball cap and gave the fence a good look. "No. I think what I said is complaining is the same as volunteering."

"Then I guess I should call Dane to help because he complained about my fence." Alex lifted the post driver again and positioned another metal fence post. "What brings you out here?"

"I don't know." He waited until Alex was finished with the post before finishing. "I guess I thought you might need to talk."

"Did you get that in a text or an email?"

Pastor Matthews laughed. "God mail."

"I guess you and about everyone else in town has seen the county paper."

Alex headed for his truck and the thermos of water he'd left on the tailgate. His gaze shifted to the bulls he'd bought. They were on a five-acre field with fences that were strong enough to hold them. They hadn't been cheap. And there was a lot of risk involved.

He should sell them. They were a dream,

but not a necessity. He told Pastor Matthews as much, expecting he'd probably agree.

"Why would you want to do that? You're just getting started. Don't you want to give it more time?" Pastor Matthews asked as he sat on the tailgate of the truck. Alex joined him.

"I don't know. It feels like I'm being shut out of the bigger events. And I can't make money if my bulls don't qualify." He shrugged it off.

"I guess that's a decision you'll have to make. And one I'd put a lot of prayer into. It's hard to trust when things aren't going the way we thought they would, or the way we planned."

"Ain't that the truth?"

Alex's gaze skimmed the ranch that his dad had bought thirty years ago. "I wish I could just walk away from this place. I have a lot of bad memories and most of them are attached to this land."

"Put it on the market and do something different."

He laughed. "What would I do, Pastor? I'm a rancher. I've spent some time in the city and I can't say I liked it much."

"What if there is something else and you're so focused on this one aspect of your life, you can't see the other path?"

"I guess I'll have to hope there's some road signs so I don't get lost. I'd just like for things to go smoothly for a change. I kind of thought this was the easy part of my life. I'm home, business is going well, I have my bulls, rebuilding the livestock on this place. And then out of the blue…"

Out of the blue came a bride standing on the side of the road looking for all the world like she'd been meant for him. But she wasn't for him. Her kind never was.

"Out of the blue?" Pastor Matthews had hopped off the end of the truck and picked up the post driver, as if he really did plan on helping with the fence.

"Out of the blue you find out your mother has put a big old mortgage on the ranch and you might lose it all."

"Don't let it get you down, Alex. It'll work out. Even if it doesn't work out the way you thought it might."

"Growing up, my dad liked to tell me to stop dreaming. He told me I'd never make it to the pros in bull riding. He told me I wouldn't amount to anything. Worthless. That was his pet name for me and Marcus."

Duncan Matthews had heard the story more than once but he still shook his head and sighed. "His voice is still in your head. But the difference is, God is in your heart and His plan is what matters. He's given you a hope and a future. So whose voice do you trust the most?"

"Good sermon, Pastor."

The sarcasm rolled off the other man and he just laughed. "Thank you, Alex. I might use that next Sunday."

"Then you won't mind if I'm not at church. Since I helped write the sermon and all."

"Oh, you should be there. I'll mention your name in the final credits." He pulled on a pair of work gloves. "Let me help you with this fence before I go."

"Thanks, I'd appreciate that."

An hour later they were pulling the fence when Duncan stepped back and wiped at the perspiration dripping down his face. "This is not easy work and I'm out of shape."

"Stick with me. I'll keep you working and get you back in shape."

"That's good of you, but I think I'll stick to my day job. Hey, by the way, how's Dan doing?"

They fastened the last section of the fence and Alex pulled off his gloves.

"He's better. Marissa is still here, helping him out."

"That's good of her. I'm sure he appreciates it."

"I don't think I'd call it appreciation. And if

he does appreciate it, he isn't going to tell her or anyone else."

"She seems like a nice girl."

At the seemingly innocent statement, Alex laughed. "I see where this is going."

Pastor Matthews looked innocent. "I'm not sure what you mean?"

"Single woman comes to town. Single man obviously needs a wife."

"I didn't know you were looking for a wife."

"I'm single and I plan on staying that way."

"Time has a way of changing things."

Alex tossed the post driver and two remaining posts in the back of the truck before answering. "That isn't changing. I know how to ride bulls. I can raise some cattle. I can train a horse. But I'm not about to follow in the footsteps of my father and ruin the lives of a woman or children."

"Alex, you aren't your father."

"No, I'm not. And I don't plan on becoming my father. Ever." Alex glanced at his watch, needing to end this conversation before it went from uncomfortable to downright aggravating. "I'm bringing the pony tomorrow and I'll be there to help with the Christmas lists."

"Again, I'd say you aren't your father. You're the real deal, Alex."

Alex reached for the jug of water in the back of his truck. "Bringing a pony to a fund-raiser for some kids to ride doesn't change much. I'm just doing what I can."

"That's all any of us can do. I'll see you tomorrow."

"Sure thing."

He watched the pastor drive away. He could admit he was pretty thankful for Duncan Matthews. The man had done a lot for the community. He'd done a lot for Alex.

Now if Alex could only make himself believe that there was a silver lining in this cloud of a situation with the ranch.

He could live without this place. He could start over on a smaller spread of his own. No matter what, he knew he'd survive the loss of the ranch.

But he wasn't sure about Marcus. Or even Maria. He couldn't let go of the ranch. Bad memories and all, it was one of the few constants in their lives.

He had a lot of plans for this place, and for the future. Marissa Walker didn't figure into those plans.

At least, that was what he told himself, even if it wasn't close to the truth.

Chapter Nine

"I don't see why I have to go to town with you," Dan grumbled as they headed for the truck late Friday afternoon. "When are you going to head back to Dallas? Or are you going to stay and nag at me for another couple of weeks?"

Marissa kept her lips pressed in a firm and disapproving line, the better to deal with her grandfather. He was right, she should be going home. With Christmas coming up and a new job to start in January, she needed to get back to life. Her life.

But lately she wondered if it had ever truly been *her* life.

"Dan, get in the truck." She opened the passenger-side door and he stood there looking at her. He scratched his grizzled chin and shook his head.

"This is my truck. Why am I getting in on the passenger side?"

"Because you haven't been cleared to drive." And because she obviously loved getting pulled over by the local cop.

Her grandfather glowered at her. But then his expression softened. "It hasn't been all bad. Having you here."

"It hasn't been all bad being here."

"It wasn't like I had a choice," her grandfather said a few minutes later, as they were driving down the road toward Bluebonnet.

Marissa gave him a quick look. "What?"

"Letting you stay. I didn't have much choice in the matter, now did I?" He cleared his throat and she waited, wondering if he could give her a final ultimatum on leaving. "Still, I'm glad we had a chance to get to know each other."

"Me, too." She drove another mile, then slowed to pull into the church parking lot. "I'm going to buy us a Christmas tree."

He brushed a hand over his unshaven face. "Now listen here, just because I said something nice doesn't mean you have the right to start hauling in your stuff. I don't want a tree. I don't have room for a tree. End of story."

"It's almost Christmas. We need a tree."

"You're going back to Dallas and then I'll have to deal with taking it down. And the mess. No, ma'am, no tree."

"The money goes to the shelter. And besides, you'll thank me when it's decorated and has lights."

"I doubt that," he grumbled. "But go ahead. Do what you want."

She got out of the truck and headed for the trees that were in a sectioned-off area of the churchyard. She didn't look back to see if Dan had followed. The sound of children laughing drew her attention to an area at the back of the church. In a round pen a man walked a gray pony carrying a little girl.

"Dad-burn-it," Dan growled. "I nearly ran into you. What in the world are you thinking, stopping like that?"

"Sorry, Granddad, I got distracted."

"Uh-huh, by Alex Palermo. No wonder you're still hanging around."

"I'm here because you're my grandfather."

"I know who I am. My lungs are bad, not my memory. Now let's get a tree. Mind you, keep it small. I don't have a lot of room."

She hooked her arm through his and he shook his head. But he also didn't pull away from her.

The trees were all sizes and shapes, already set up in tree stands. Marissa led her grandfather to a tree that stood about three feet tall. It wasn't overly round and it had a nice shape.

"This one," she told him.

"If that's the one you want." He pulled out his billfold.

"I'll buy it."

"Don't argue with me. It's my tree and my house." He pulled away from her. "Dane Scott, I'm here to buy a tree."

The man her grandfather approached was in his early thirties. He was tall and had a genuine smile as he greeted Dan.

"Having a woman around will make a man change his ways, Dan."

"Don't I know it." Her grandfather shot her an amused look. "One week almost and she's had me in the hospital and now cluttering the place up with a Christmas tree."

Dane laughed. "But you love it and don't deny it."

Her grandfather didn't deny it. Granddad grumbled that Dane could help put the tree in the back of the truck.

"Come on," her grandfather said as he walked past her. "I guess we might as well see what else is going on. You're a little old but I reckon I can take you to the pony rides. Seems that's what a grandfather should do."

"I'm a little too big for pony rides but you can buy me a burger." She pointed to the concession stand.

"That'll make my cholesterol go up."

"It's for a good cause. The money is for the women's shelter. The money they earn today will help buy Christmas gifts for these children and other needy families."

"I know what the money is for." Dan headed for the pony rides. "Come on. We have twenty-six years of lost time to make up for."

She followed her grandfather, her feet dragging. He'd somehow managed to turn the tables on her. When she reached the pony ride, there were only a few children waiting. Her grandfather got in line.

The children and the two moms present gave them curious looks and then whispered behind their hands. The little girl in front of Dan reached for his hand and gave it a tug.

"Hey, aren't you too big to ride a pony?" The little girl wrinkled her nose at Marissa's grandfather and then squinted as she looked at Marissa.

"My granddaughter has never ridden a pony," Dan told the child in a much kinder tone than he'd ever used with Marissa. "And if you're nice, I'll pay for you to ride that pony twice."

"Really? Twice?" The child beamed with happiness.

Dan nodded and handed her the money. "Merry Christmas."

The child pulled on his hand and motioned

him to her level. When Dan leaned down, the little girl gave him a quick hug. "Thank you."

"You're welcome," he said in a voice thick with emotion. "It's not like it's a big deal."

"To her it is," Marissa countered. "You're a big softy. But I won't tell."

They waited ten minutes in line. Marissa kept her gaze averted so that she didn't make eye contact with Alex. She talked to her grandfather. She talked to the child, whose name was Joy, and then to the mom, Hanna, and her daughter, Amy, who got in line behind them.

She allowed the children to move ahead of her in the line.

Finally they were at the front of the line. She had no intention of getting on the tiny pony that Alex held as he looked at them. His hand went to the gray neck of the pony. He studied them with his hat pulled low. Ever so slowly he shook his head, and white teeth flashed as the corners of his mouth tugged up.

"Dan, the pony ride is for kids."

Dan looked from the pony to Marissa and back to the pony. Marissa put a hand on his arm. She'd gone along with the silliness. Now she felt even more.

"Dan, really, we both know I can't ride that pony."

"I know but I liked the idea of it." He looked

away but not before she saw a shimmer of moisture in his eyes. "It's what I would have done…"

"Yes, I know."

Alex patted her grandfather on the back. "Give me five minutes, Dan. I think I can solve this problem."

Marissa wanted to walk away. The last thing she wanted to do was stand there looking conspicuous while her grandfather smiled as if he'd just scored a major victory.

When her grandfather chuckled she shot him a questioning look. "What's so funny?"

"You," he replied. "That is not a happy look on your face. I got you a pony ride. I don't see why you're so upset."

"I didn't want a pony ride," she told him. "I'm doing this for you."

"And I'm doing this for you. You'll either thank me. Or you'll thank me to stay out of your business."

She was being taught a lesson. On meddling. And for some reason, rather than being put out, she was amused. Her grandfather's blue eyes twinkled as he watched her. When he winked, she laughed.

"You're impossible."

He laughed a little harder. "That's what your grandmother told me the entire twelve years of our marriage."

"I wish…" she began. But she didn't know how to continue. He must have known because he shifted uncomfortably and let out a long sigh.

"She had good reasons for leaving, so don't wish for something that wouldn't have done anyone any good."

"But she could have let my mother see you," she said.

"I wasn't much of a husband. Or much of a father. I drank too much. I cared too little. Until they were gone. Later on I cared a lot, but it was too late. Your mother was better off without me."

"I'm sorry," she told him. Briefly she leaned her head against his shoulder and she wondered what life might have been like had he been in their world. He would have been gruff but he would have spoken the truth. Maybe he would have prodded them all into living their lives and not wallowing in the grief after the loss of her sister.

"I've never been more sorry than now," he answered. "And I mean that, Marissa. I really do wish I'd been there for you all."

She wiped at tears rolling down her cheeks. She wished he'd been there, too. Because at times it had seemed that everyone had someone to lean on. And she'd been left with no one. Her parents had leaned on each other. Her grandmother had leaned on friends. Marissa had been a child alone.

After the near miss of a wedding, she realized she would have continued to have no one if she'd married Aidan. Not once in the entire time they'd been dating had she ever shared with him how much it had hurt to lose her sister. She hadn't confided how she'd always felt guilty. She hadn't shared anything of her struggles with him.

Alex was lifting a child off the pony and talking to her about the little horse he called Cobalt. The mother thanked him. He watched them walk away and then focused his attention on Dan and Marissa. She wondered what he thought of them.

Because she wanted to confide in him. She wanted to tell him things about herself and about her new job that she didn't really want.

She pushed away the thoughts because this wasn't home and could never be home. She knew that.

Still, it never hurt to dream, did it?

Alex checked himself before he tied Cobalt and headed for Dan and Marissa. She had that hurt expression on her face. As much as he wanted to ask her what was wrong, he knew he couldn't. She wasn't his problem. If he knew what had put that look on her face, he'd want to know more. To help her. He was already all kinds of involved, he didn't want to get even more involved. The sooner she hightailed it back to Dallas, the better.

"Well, Palermo, tell us why we've been standing here waiting for you," Old Dan grouched in his customary tone. Most people were put off by Dan. Alex wasn't. He'd seen the older man take in too many strays. He'd also seen the kindness in his eyes when he asked questions.

More than once in Alex's life, Dan had given him a stern talking-to about living in the past and how it did a man no good to dwell on mistakes made. Better to make wiser choices in the future and keep moving forward, Dan had told him.

"I have a pony more Marissa's size." Alex took her by the hand, the gesture a little too easy, and led her to his truck and trailer. He'd put up a few panels and penned his horse, Bolt. "I brought him with me today because he needs to hang out with crowds."

Bolt was a pale cream, almost white. He had crazy eyes but a good disposition. Alex had learned not to judge a horse by the eyes.

"That horse isn't going to throw my granddaughter, is he?" Dan asked, stepping close to take a good look at Bolt.

"I wouldn't let her on him if I thought he

would throw her," Alex answered as he stepped inside the pen with the horse.

Bolt stood still as Alex slid the bridle on and then saddled him. He adjusted the stirrups, tightened the cinch and led the horse out. All this time he'd been avoiding eye contact with Marissa. Now he could no longer avoid it. She had backed a few steps away from the horse and her blue eyes were wide.

"Don't tell me you're afraid of this one, too?"

"Has she seen any other?" Dan asked, his eyes narrowing as he looked from one to the other of them.

"Yeah, the other day I rode over to your place." Alex had tossed out the comment with a casual shrug. Dan didn't look happy.

It seemed wise to move on. "You ready for your pony ride?"

She stepped forward.

Alex stepped around the front of the horse. "You're on the wrong side."

"Oh." She eased around the front of the horse.

He circled her wrist with his hand. It was a small wrist. She gave him a look and he cleared his throat and remembered that he was letting her have a belated pony ride. He glanced at Dan. "This is going to cost you five dollars for the shelter fund."

"I'll write the preacher a check," Dan said with a twinkle in his faded blue eyes.

"Left foot in the stirrup."

She lifted her left foot.

"Grab hold of the saddle horn and pull yourself up."

She did, but with a struggle. He smiled as she settled on the saddle, looking a little apprehensive as she bit down on her bottom lip. He handed her the reins and she took them in hands that appeared to shake. And then, before he could take hold of the bridle, she gave Bolt a nudge with her heel and shot forward.

"Hey," he yelled as she took off.

She glanced back, laughing. "Summer camp. Every year since I was five."

Dan slapped his leg and chortled. "I guess she showed you."

Alex glared at the older man. "This is going to cost you more than five bucks, Dan."

"I kind of figured. But in my defense, I didn't know she could ride."

Alex went after the woman and his horse. She had slowed to a walk. He whistled. Bolt immediately stopped. Four hooves planted in the dusty yard of the church as the horse looked back at him.

"I'm guessing summer camp didn't teach her

that." Alex walked fast, not convinced the horse would really stay.

"That wasn't fair," Marissa called out. She was beaming, though, and her blue eyes flashed with humor.

"Neither was pretending you needed a pony ride." Alex caught hold of the reins. "Move your foot."

She eased her left foot from the stirrup. He claimed it and swung up behind her, letting her keep the seat. His arms were around her as he guided the horse in the direction of an open field across the dirt road at the back of the church.

"We shouldn't do this," she said over her shoulder.

"Probably not. There are probably dozens of reasons this is a bad idea. But you started it."

Her dark hair was in his face, the scent something tropical and sweet. He leaned in a little, so that his chin was on her shoulder and his arms were around her as he held the reins. She was dangerous. She was beautiful. There were so many reasons he shouldn't want to be around this woman.

He tried to list them off for himself, hoping it would help him keep perspective.

She could ride a horse but she was still a city girl.

She'd go back to Dallas and he'd still be in

Bluebonnet, living his dreams that were nothing like what a woman in her world dreamed of.

She had been let down by the man she was supposed to spend her life with, and he didn't want to be another man who let her down.

But there was one big, fat, undeniable truth. When he held her in his arms, it felt like a promise.

"Where are we going?" Her voice was soft when she asked the question.

They were riding along a line of trees, the shade cool. In the distance he could hear children laughing and a car honk. When he glanced back, he saw Dan still standing by the horse trailer.

"We won't go far," he assured her.

She shivered and he held her a little closer.

"We shouldn't do this." Hers was the voice of reason, soft and sweet and way too tempting to be reasonable.

It took him a minute to decide what she meant. They shouldn't ride away from the church? Or they shouldn't be tempted? He realized she meant riding away, together, alone.

"No, we shouldn't," he agreed.

But her hair blew against his cheek and he came a bit closer. His lips grazed her cheek. When she turned to say something, he kissed the corner of her mouth. Her eyes closed and she whispered his name. She should have told him to stop. She didn't.

He pulled back on the reins and Bolt stopped. He slid off the back of the horse and walked around to take hold of the reins. He reached up and Marissa took his hand, wary, as she should be. Watching him, she brought her leg over the horse's neck, slid her left foot from the stirrup and jumped. He caught her, holding her loosely with one arm.

"We shouldn't," he whispered against the soft skin of her cheek. His hand had moved to her hair, finding it soft and silky in his fingers.

"No," she agreed. But she stood on tiptoe and her mouth captured his.

Slow down, he told himself. *Think things through*. Slow and steady, no one gets hurt. But she tasted sweet, like coffee and sugar and everything wonderful.

She tasted like forever. Someone else's forever. She was subdivisions, picket fences and a husband in a suit. He was one month away from losing the family ranch if he didn't make quick decisions and find cash.

He pulled back. Her eyes were closed, her dark lashes brushing her ivory skin. He kissed each cheek, feeling the flutter of those lashes on his lips.

"I can't imagine…" he began, but cut himself

off. He couldn't imagine a man walking away from her.

"What?" Her head was on his shoulder. She took a deep breath, her shoulders rising and falling.

"Nothing. We should go."

She stepped away from him in silent agreement and remounted the horse. He handed her the reins and then, with one hand on the horn and the other on the back of the saddle, he swung his right leg over Bolt's back and settled behind her.

As they rode back to the church he told himself he'd made a mistake that he wouldn't make again. And then he disagreed with himself. The man who had walked away from her had made a mistake.

She wasn't a mistake. She was just out of his league.

And he was nowhere near the ballpark.

Chapter Ten

Marissa fought the urge to lean back into Alex's arms. That would be a mistake. But these days she seemed to be an expert at making mistakes. She closed her eyes just briefly. What she needed was to go home, back to Dallas.

To what? Humiliation? Disappointed parents?

She opened her eyes and saw her grandfather sitting in the passenger side of Alex's truck. He stepped out as they got closer and she could see the worry on his expression. He looked protective. The look took her by surprise.

"I'm sorry," Alex whispered as they got closer.

She couldn't let him take the blame. "I'm the one that took off on your horse. I…"

And she had initiated the kiss, hadn't she?

"Don't overthink it," Alex said. His hand was warm on hers.

"Right. Of course." She didn't wait for his

help. She slipped her right leg over the horse's neck and slid to the ground. Bolt gave her a curious look but didn't seem too offended by the awkward dismount.

Her grandfather joined them. The glare he gave Alex was long and hard. She was sure a lesser man would have been shaking in his boots. "The preacher asked me to bring her on in. He'd like to show her around the shelter."

Alex rested a hand on Bolt's neck. He nodded but he didn't say anything as she walked away with Dan. They entered the church through a back entrance into the large kitchen and fellowship hall. There were women in the kitchen and children gathered around a tree that reached the ceiling of the dining room.

Pastor Matthews approached, his face split in a friendly greeting. "Hey, good to see the two of you. I saw you picking a tree and when you didn't come inside I thought you'd left. And, Dan, I know you don't want to miss this chili or the pies. All of this is a fund-raiser for the shelter as well as helping families in the community."

"I guess I'm already owing you money for the tree and pony ride."

"Well, come on in and we'll see what else you might want," the pastor said. "Marissa, good to see you again. I'm not sure if you'd be interested but the kids are looking for someone to help them decorate the tree."

There were half a dozen small children and a plastic tub full of decorations. Marissa nodded and headed for the Christmas tree. Pastor Matthews followed.

"Kids, this is Marissa. She's going to help you with the tree. All of you remember your manners and be respectful."

"Yes, sir," one little boy said, and saluted. "She can't reach the top of the tree, though."

The pastor chuckled. "Well, she can reach most of the tree. I'll send someone to help with the higher branches."

He left and she was alone with the children. They were immediately curious. But she was in her element; she knew how to talk to them.

They showed her the popcorn and cranberries they were stringing. Together they sat in a circle sharing stories about favorite pets, what they wanted for Christmas and things they missed.

And that was the part that hurt. A little girl named Julie poked the needle through a cranberry, then popcorn. She had sad brown eyes and she told Marissa she missed her cat, Zippy. Zippy used to sleep with her but that was a long time ago, when her mom and dad still lived together.

"I haven't seen Zippy since we left." Julie drew in a breath but she didn't cry.

"We had to give our pets away," Amy from the pony ride told Marissa. "We didn't have electricity for a long time and my mom said we couldn't have our puppy because food was too expensive and we needed electricity for heat. But then we moved here."

The stories went on and on. There shouldn't be so many children with such heartbreaking stories.

When the cranberries and popcorn were finally strung, they lifted the strings and together wrapped them around the tree. The children played and laughed as they worked and Marissa smiled easier than she'd smiled in days.

"We should hang the rest of the decorations on the tree and then we'll plug in the lights." Marissa pulled the tub of decorations to the center of the children.

Amy pulled out a manger scene painted on a bulb shaped like a star. "I like this one the best. It's the story of Christmas."

A little boy named Timmy leaned close and then looked up with a sweet expression on his face. "Pastor Matthews says it's the story of hope."

"What does hope mean?" Marissa knelt down in front of the child.

"Hope is the evidence of things unseen. We learned that in Sunday school," Julie said brightly. "And I think that must be about trusting God even when we can't see Him."

Amy tugged on Marissa's arm. "Because God always has a plan. That's what Pastor Matthews said. He said we aren't supposed to worry. We're supposed to let God and the grown-ups handle the problems."

Marissa hadn't been to church in years, but sitting here with these children, her own hope was renewed. Timmy handed her the star ornament. "Do you believe in Christmas?"

She nodded, but her heart ached at the question because these children had been through so much and yet they were still smiling. They were finding faith. And hope.

No child should ever be without hope.

Marissa couldn't help but be touched by the children, their stories, their joy. She hadn't experienced anything like this in a long time. Maybe ever.

"How's it going over here?" Alex appeared at her side. He'd taken off his hat and his dark curls were flattened against his head. With a glance he took in the children, the tree and the decoration in her hand.

Timmy reached into the tub of decorations. "We're doing great. And the tree is beautiful."

The little boy pulled out a book and handed it to Marissa.

"Will you read it?" he asked.

She took the book. Of course they would want a story. She touched the cover before opening it to look at the beautiful illustrations inside. Alex was watching. He would wonder why she hesitated. He wouldn't understand.

Worse, what would he say if he knew her secret? Would he make a joke of it as Aidan had, and then pretend the teasing was in good fun? Would he be embarrassed for her?

The children were looking on with expectant faces. Hopeful. And she wouldn't let them down. She couldn't let her own insecurities dampen what they had found. Hope.

They all believed so strongly in the story of Christmas and the hope of things unseen.

"'Joseph took Mary, who was great with child.'" She smiled at the children and then her eyes misted as she touched the words, the pictures. She told the story as she remembered it. "And went to Bethlehem. And while they were there, the time came for the baby to be born. She wrapped him in warm cloths and lay him in the manger. There was no room in the inn.

"'At the same time there were shepherds in a field.'" She smiled at the children. They'd moved closer. "'Watching over their sheep.'

"'And there appeared in the sky an Angel of the Lord saying, "For unto you is born this day in the city of David, a Savior who is Christ the Lord. And this will be a sign unto you. You will find the baby wrapped in swaddling clothes and lying in a manger.'"

She took a deep breath and looked up, catching Alex's gaze on her. His eyes were warm chocolate and his lips tilted up as he winked at her. If Aidan hadn't left, she never would have known this about herself, that she wanted a man who made her feel strong. And special. And Aidan hadn't ever been that man.

"It isn't over, is it?" Julie asked. She was six, she'd told Marissa. And her mommy was having a baby.

"No, it isn't over." Pastor Matthews appeared. "The story continues through us and through our faith. But right now, it's time for you all to eat. And maybe Miss Marissa can come back again."

"I would love to come back. I loved spending time with you all."

"Be careful," Alex warned. "Pastor Matthews is always looking for volunteers."

"I won't be here long," she told him. "But I'd love to help when I can."

The children hugged her and then they were gone, laughing and telling how they'd decorated the tree and talked about hope. Pastor Matthews's voice rose above theirs as he told them only one person could talk at a time. And then they disappeared into the kitchen. Marissa stood by the tree, alone with Alex.

"I'm dyslexic," she said before he could ask. "So no, I wasn't reading all of the words. I can read. But at times the words seem to bounce. Or they're jumbled."

"I wondered. My twin brother is dyslexic." He studied her face. "You're a teacher. That couldn't have been easy."

"It wasn't." She wanted to hug him. She wanted to grab him and thank him. She couldn't put into words how his statement, making it an accomplishment, making it matter, made her feel.

It hadn't been easy, to put aside her fears and pursue a career she had wanted and that she loved. It still wasn't always easy to pursue what she wanted. Not when there might be rejection at the end of the chase.

Several days after the fund-raiser, Alex walked through the house, the very empty house. He couldn't wait for Maria to arrive. At least she would make a mess or play her music too loud. Even Marcus would be preferable to the silence. Maria wouldn't be home for another week or so. He wasn't sure about Marcus.

It hadn't always been this way. Growing up it had been a full house. Alex, his twin brother, their sisters and parents. Their dad had been loud and rarely peaceful. The house hadn't been a place any of them ever wanted to be, but it had been their home. Sometimes there had even been laughter.

Alex had no intentions of making it a home again. His goal was to build his own place, just big enough for him. He didn't need more. Marcus or Maria could have this house and do what they wanted with it. He needed no reminders of their past.

But first, he had to get the loan. He needed cash.

The light on the kitchen phone blinked, letting him know someone had left a message. He pushed the button and put the phone on speaker before playing the messages. The third one made him stop. He had to replay it. Twice.

His bulls had been accepted for a charity bull ride. He glanced at the calendar. Not a lot of money to be made but it would add to his points. And he desperately needed to make points in order to get the bulls into the bigger events. He said a quiet thank-you because he had needed something good to happen.

Not only would the money be good, but it would also be time away from Bluebonnet. He scrubbed a hand over his face as he contemplated the contents of his fridge. Nothing looked decent. Most of it probably needed to be tossed out.

He wondered what Marissa and Dan were having for dinner. Yeah, that's why he needed to get away from Bluebonnet for a few days. He didn't have time to be distracted. He grabbed a package of ham out of the fridge and a loaf of bread that wasn't so stale he couldn't eat it.

The phone rang. He let it go to voice mail.

It rang again. He picked it up.

"Hello," he said as he put ham on a slice of bread.

"Alex, its Marissa. I need help over here."

"Another cow down?" He glanced out the window. It was starting to rain and the thermometer read fifty degrees. He was a good neighbor but he sure didn't want to go pull a calf in this weather.

"There's someone here with a stock trailer. They're claiming they're from the IRS and Dan said that because he didn't have the money to pay back taxes, they can have half a dozen head of cattle. You and I both know that the IRS doesn't work that way."

"I'll call 911. And don't argue with them. They're cattle thieves, plain and simple, and you don't know what they might do." As he gave the warning, he realized just how true it was and how much danger she was in. But he also knew she wouldn't sit back and do nothing.

Dread settled in the pit of his stomach as he ended the call and dialed 911. He gave the details and Dan's address. They tried to tell him to stay clear and let them handle the situation. He couldn't do that.

He couldn't sit at his house eating a ham sandwich while Dan and his granddaughter faced off with what were probably armed cattle thieves who had found a new way to rob an old man blind.

He tossed the sandwich to his sister's poodle and headed out the door, jamming his hat on his head as he went. Leave it to Dan to fall for something as crazy as an IRS scam. What made a normally intelligent person think that something such as this was legit?

When he got to Dan's, Marissa, wearing a rain parka, stood in the muddy yard hugging herself tight and staring out toward the field. Dusk had fallen and the gray sky was going to be dark soon. He jumped out of his truck. She shifted to look at him, shaking her head. Drops of rain sprayed from the parka.

"They insisted on Granddad getting in the truck with them. I told him to stay but he wouldn't. That's when he told me to call you. I hope they didn't hear him."

"I hope so, too." He put an arm around her and she shivered, tucking herself close to his side. When she leaned into him like that, he wanted to be the man who didn't let her down. He wanted to make things right for her.

He shook off those dangerous thoughts. "Go inside the camper. When the deputies get here, tell them I'm down there pretending to help load cattle. I want to make sure Dan is okay."

"You shouldn't."

"I know. But I can't leave Dan down there alone. They probably didn't count on you being here so they're probably a little on the nervous side. Hopefully the deputies don't come in here with sirens blaring." He gave her a gentle nudge toward the camper. "Go."

She nodded and walked away from him, but her gaze kept traveling back to the field and to headlights in the distance. Cattle mooed and he could hear men shouting. He wished he'd done something sooner, like the first time Dan mentioned the IRS. But at the time Dan hadn't mentioned the details, just that he owed money.

The door to the camper closed with a click. He headed back to his truck.

He found Dan and the cattle thieves at the back of the property. They'd brought four-wheelers and they were loading cattle. Dan stood off to the side with one of the men. He looked a little gray and even from a distance it appeared he was trying to catch his breath.

Alex parked his truck and got out. He gave the men a friendly, helpful smile and waved. "Hey, I thought I might come out and help you all. This rain is getting worse."

"Sir, I'm going to ask you to stand back." The fake agent in his fake black jacket pulled a handgun from his pocket.

Alex had never thought himself a fool and he wasn't going to be one today. He raised his hands. "Hey, I'm not here to cause any trouble. I just wanted to help. It would be a shame if you all got that truck stuck out here, and the way this rain is coming down, that's a possibility."

The men—there were four of them—looked at each other. The one who still had his handgun fixed on Alex shook his head. "No, I think we can manage. Go ahead and get back in your truck."

"How about if I take Dan off your hands. It looks like he's about to pass out on you. He's got some heart problems. Dan, do you have your heart medicine on you?"

Dan looked a little confused and shook his head. "No."

"You're a little pale. Why don't you go sit in the truck?" Alex kept his hands up and a smile on his face. Maybe he was a fool because the more he pushed, the more the thug with the gun looked as if he might like to unload some lead in him.

As if on cue, Dan weaved a little and he reached for the man next to him to steady himself.

"Get off me, old man."

No way would an IRS agent talk like that. Alex thought about mentioning it but kept his mouth shut. All those people who said he didn't know when to shut up would have been surprised.

"Dan, you okay?"

The guy with the gun pointed the weapon at Alex. "Get back in your truck and take him with you. But don't try to leave. Just sit there and stay out of the way."

Dan headed his way at a snail's pace.

"Dan, why don't you try to hurry and we'll get out of the rain?"

"I'm going as fast as I can, Alex. I don't know why you're over here getting in my business. I owe the IRS and I'm taking care of my debt."

Alex opened the passenger seat of the truck.

"I hope you know these men aren't IRS," he whispered.

"Well, I kind of figured that out. And that's why I didn't offer them what I have in my safe."

Alex swallowed a chuckle and closed the door.

As he went around to the driver's side he heard cars in the distance. He moved a little quicker. He was behind the wheel and closing the door when the first shot rang out.

"They're shooting at my truck. Now that just makes a guy mad. Dan, stay down." He floored it and headed for the nearest four-wheeler, making the guy spin the thing and almost go sideways in the mud. With that one close to disabled, Alex turned and headed back toward the gate.

He pulled to the side as deputies in SUVs headed through the gate. As they slowed, he rolled down the window. The first vehicle stopped.

"They're armed. They have a truck and trailer and a couple of ATVs."

After that he headed back to the camper with Dan, who was having a hard time catching his breath. "You know you're supposed to use that oxygen. You're just being stubborn. Imagine how much better you'd feel if you used it."

"Oh, stop. Now you sound like Marissa. What I'd really like is if she'd go back to Dallas and you'd go back to minding your own business."

"And leave you to lose your life savings to fake IRS agents?"

"Well, I do appreciate your help. But not your advice on my health. I'm seventy-five and the last thing I want is to have a couple of kids telling me how to live. She's making me eat oatmeal in the mornings. And juice. 'Drink water,' she says. 'Cut back on coffee,' she says.'"

Alex laughed as he pulled his truck up to the steps of the camper. "You know you love her."

"I know I do." Dan gave him a meaningful look.

"Don't look at me like that, Dan. She's your granddaughter, not mine. And I don't have any intention of getting tangled up with a city girl on the rebound who won't be here long enough for me to know her favorite color."

"Come on in. She'll make us a cup of that herbal tea she's so dad-burned fond of."

Alex followed Dan up the stairs. The door opened as they got to the top and Marissa was waiting. She hugged her grandfather as she pulled him inside. Before Dan could protest, she had a towel around him and she was drying his hair. The older man grumbled but he put up with her ministrations. He even turned a little pink when she kissed his cheek.

"Sit down and I'll get you something warm to drink."

"I guess it's too much to hope for a cup of coffee?" Dan asked with a hopeful tone.

"No coffee this late at night. But I made some ginger tea."

Dan groaned but he took a seat in his old recliner and put his feet up. Alex grabbed the oxygen tank and pulled it to Dan.

"Use this thing."

Dan took the tubing, adjusted the knobs and gave Alex a look that didn't need much interpretation. When Alex moved back a step, Marissa was there with a towel.

"Dry off," she said, handing it to him. Her eyes searched his face. He didn't know what she was looking for, but he hoped she didn't look too deep.

He took the towel, dried his face and hair and handed it back to her. "I'll wait until the police are finished. Do you need anything done while I'm here?"

"No. The chores are all done."

"Good grief, this is enough to make a man feel a little sick," Dan grumbled, capturing both of their attention.

"What?" Marissa asked. Alex could have told her asking was a mistake.

Dan pointed from her to Alex and back to her. He wrinkled up his nose. "This. The cooing. And the looks. He's a confirmed bachelor. He just told me a month ago that he thinks women are more trouble than they're worth. And you, you just got jilted by your fiancé. Why would you even think of trusting another man?"

"I'm just being nice to a neighbor who helped

us out." Marissa wagged her finger at her grandfather. "You're just being testy because I've cut you back on coffee and sugar. And because we're having baked chicken for dinner and not fried."

"I like baked chicken," Alex said to no one in particular. After all, he'd tossed his sandwich to a dog when he'd left the house.

"You can have mine," Dan told him. "I'm having bologna. And I think in a month or two, you'll both be eating crow."

"I'm not a fan of crow," Alex said. Fortunately the police chose that moment to knock on the door.

Marissa peeked through the window, then opened the door to let in a couple of rain-soaked deputies. They had a few questions for Dan and Alex, but the thieves were in custody and there would be several charges filed against them.

Alex stepped into the small kitchen area as they questioned Dan. Marissa joined him. She avoided looking at him and he guessed he might have been avoiding her. She pulled the chicken from the oven and took the lid off a pan with some kind of cheesy potatoes.

"You'll stay for dinner?" she asked.

"I wouldn't mind." He moved close—close enough to smell the soft floral scent of her perfume, close enough to hear her quickly indrawn breath. He touched his fingers to her, just briefly. "You're okay?"

"I'm okay."

"You know he was just teasing." He'd felt compelled to say it.

"I know."

She looked at him then and he felt a tightness in his chest. The vulnerable softness in her blue eyes begged him not to hurt her.

He wanted more than anything to be the man who wouldn't let her down.

Chapter Eleven

By Saturday morning Marissa thought things were settling down nicely. Including her grandfather, and her nerves. They were in a groove, she and Dan. They'd dealt with several visits by the police. They'd had a lot of questions about the past six months, how much had been taken and how many head of cattle Dan had turned over to the men. Because of the police report, Dan would be able to file insurance claims and be reimbursed for his loss. In all he'd given up over twenty head of cattle without ever questioning the men or their motives.

The police had taken Marissa aside and told her that it was a new scam, but not surprising that they targeted her grandfather. Dan lived alone, with no family that checked in on him, and he was older, therefore the crooks figured he was an easy mark. Fortunately Marissa had come along when she did.

She could have told them it had been fortunate for her, too.

With the church potluck taking place the next day, Marissa had plans to make deviled eggs. And she also needed to plan her exit from Bluebonnet Springs.

She peeked in the nesting box in the dimly lit henhouse, pulled out an egg and placed it in the basket. She reached in the next box and a sharp beak pecked at her hand. The hen squawked a warning a little too late. A nester. Her grandfather had warned her that a few of the hens were determined to sit on their nests and to just leave them be.

At least she hadn't dropped the basket of eggs.

"Fine, have your eggs." She counted the green and brown eggs in the basket. Almost a dozen. That was perfect. With the dozen in the house she could make a couple dozen deviled eggs for the potluck.

She left the chicken coop and headed across the yard, avoiding puddles that had formed from the rain the previous day. As she walked up the steps the rooster flew to the rail. He lowered his head and rounded his back.

"Now aren't you sweet." She gave him a couple of pats to his softly feathered back.

In the distance she heard a vehicle and then saw Alex's truck come up the drive. She waited for him to park. It took him a minute to get out. When he did he had two brown paper bags in his hands. He grinned and inclined his head in greeting. Even from a distance she knew his eyes would flash with humor and dimples would crease his cheeks.

"What are you doing?" she asked as he headed her way.

"Baking pies. Remember?"

He had mentioned that. She thought in jest. She should have known he wasn't joking.

"I see. You're baking them here?"

"Yep." He came up the stairs. The rooster flew off the rail and glided to a safe spot a short distance away.

"Come on in. But hopefully you really do know what you're doing. Because I don't."

He gave her a long look and then he winked. "I know what I'm doing."

Without warning he kissed her cheek.

As if that kiss hadn't mattered, he stomped the mud off his shoes and followed her inside. Marissa hurried to put the eggs away. Or to escape his nearness. He followed at a slower pace. Her grandfather was making himself a peanut butter sandwich. He turned as they entered the camper.

"Stop making a pet out of my rooster," he

grumbled as he put the lid on the peanut butter. "Did you see her out there, petting Red?"

"I did, Dan. I don't know if I would put up with that."

"Don't see as I have much choice in the matter. She doesn't seem to be going anywhere anytime soon."

Marissa gave her grandfather a quick hug. "You'd miss me if I left."

"I might at that." He kissed the top of her head.

Every day that she stayed was a day she got closer to her grandfather, and she regretted that she'd missed out on so many years. With each passing day, her desire to go home dwindled. She didn't know what awaited her back in Dallas. But she also didn't know what a future in Bluebonnet Springs would hold for her, either.

In the tiny kitchen she became aware of the other reason she wasn't excited about going home. Alex. He moved past her, their arms barely touching as he set his baking supplies on the tiny table. When he turned she swallowed because they were face-to-face, and with her grandfather in the kitchen, there was no room to move.

She and Aidan had never done anything quite as intimate as sharing space in a kitchen, cooking together. Or even doing chores together.

They'd dated. Dinners. Work functions. Movies. She had thought about it often in the past weeks. They hadn't really known each other. She hadn't known his friends. He hadn't known that she didn't want to live in an apartment. She wanted a small house in a neighborhood where they would have a fenced yard and children.

Now she'd expanded that to house in a small town and maybe some land. Because this time with her grandfather had opened her eyes to some new experiences, and to a part of herself she hadn't known.

"Nice tree," Alex said, dragging her back to the present.

She glanced at the scraggly tree they'd hauled home from the church fund-raiser. "It needs more ornaments. I found one box at the thrift store in town. It was all she had."

"Before you start on those pies, why don't you go to the barn and get what I have out there?" Dan suggested as he sat down in his recliner, a plate in his lap and a glass of milk on the table next to him. He reached for the remote. "I'm going to watch sports for a bit and maybe take a nap. If the rats haven't eaten everything, the decorations are in the attic over the feed room of the barn."

Alex glanced at her and lifted a shoulder. "I don't mind helping."

"Are you sure?"

"Come on. Get a jacket and let's get that poor tree decorated before it gets repossessed by Charlie Brown."

"It isn't that bad."

"It's worse." He grabbed her jacket off the coatrack and held it out for her.

The rain started as they headed across the yard to the barn. It was a light rain but cold. Marissa huddled into her jacket and Alex's arm went around her. The rain picked up. They ran the rest of the way, laughing as they hurried through the door.

The barn was dark and dusty, and smelled of hay, horses and cattle. Marissa found she liked the quiet and the smell. It was comforting and peaceful.

"Where is the attic?"

"This way." Alex took her hand and led her to the feed room. Inside was a ladder. He opened it beneath a square door in the ceiling.

"We have to go up there?" She eyed the opening and shook her head at the idea of climbing through and into the dark attic space.

"Yeah. Up there. Follow me."

"What if there are bugs?"

"And mice?" he asked.

"Stop."

He was already up the ladder and pushing the

square door open. She watched from below as he disappeared into the dark hole. A light came on and he peeked down at her.

"No bugs. No mice. Come on up."

She eased up the ladder, trying to keep her eyes on the man above her and not the floor below. He reached and she gave him her hand. With his help she climbed through the opening and landed safely on the floor of the attic. Tubs lined the wall. Each was labeled. There were Christmas ornaments. Photographs. Important papers. There was even a fireproof box.

"He's kept everything." Marissa stood, the ceiling just inches above her head. Alex had to duck in the confined space.

"Well, where do you want to start?"

"Christmas decorations. But I want to look in the other boxes." She reached for one of the tubs that had been taped to seal the lid. "It's funny that these boxes contain the history of my family, of people I didn't know existed."

"So we aren't getting the Christmas decorations and leaving, are we?" He gave her a hopeful smile.

"No, we aren't."

"Why would he keep this up here?" he asked, pushing the fireproof box with his foot.

"Because he's Dan and it makes sense that if he's going to get robbed, they wouldn't look in the attic of the barn. Or even think that a barn would have an attic."

"I guess you're right."

She pulled the tape and removed the lid of the first tub. Inside were family photos. Some appeared to be from when her mother was a child. Some were older than that. She picked up one of a little girl with dark hair. On the back in faded ink were the words *Mary, age five. Kindergarten.*

"My mother," she told Alex.

The next photograph was of her grandparents on their wedding day. Alex peered over her shoulder.

"Dan was a charmer."

"Yes," she agreed. "He still is."

Alex laughed. "If cranky is the new charming."

Alex reached for a newspaper clipping. Marissa leaned to see what the article was about and suddenly she couldn't breathe. She shook her head, reaching for the aged piece of paper.

"Marissa?" Alex sat down next to her.

Her fingers shook as she held the bit of paper. Alex leaned close to read the story as she blinked to make sense of the words. Seeing it in print, it all came back to her. A twelve-year-old girl was killed. Witnesses said the two children tried to cross a busy intersection. One was hit by an oncoming car. She shook her head, trying to block the image, the pain.

The loss.

Alex reached for her but she couldn't let him hold her. She'd fall apart if he touched her. She'd shatter. She could already feel the pieces coming apart as she stood there holding the article. He took it from her hands.

"You?"

She nodded at the question.

And then, without asking, he held her. And the pieces that had been shattered for so long seemed to shift. Instead of scattering she felt something else, something she hadn't expected. In the arms of this man she felt more whole than she'd felt in years. Her heart still ached with loss, with memories, but his arms around her were strong and she felt strong because of them.

She remembered all of those years ago, standing on the sidewalk, alone. It had become a trend. She'd stood to the side at the funeral. Alone. Her parents had held each other. She'd wrapped arms around herself and cried.

Her grandfather had kept the article from the paper. It had gone in the tub with pictures of a wife who had left him, a daughter he didn't really know and grandchildren he'd never met. He'd been alone, too. She wiped at her eyes and removed herself from the comfort of Alex's arms.

She wondered if her grandfather had cried over that newspaper clipping. Did he sometimes come up here and go through these memories, piece by piece.

"You're okay," he said.

The way he said it, it wasn't a question. It was a statement. She was okay.

"I'm okay." She looked at the picture of a smiling Lisa, just twelve years old. "I miss her. My family hasn't been whole since…"

She shook her head.

"Since she died." He'd supplied the difficult words and she realized his arm was still around her. She still leaned against him. How was it possible that she'd miss this man she'd known only weeks, and she didn't really miss the fiancé who had left her?

"Yes. My parents haven't been the same. It's as if life stopped. Happiness and laughter ended. Remember when we talked about Christmas for my family? It's as if we avoided the holiday because it brought back memories of that first Christmas after we lost her."

"You weren't responsible." He said the words that a few friends had tried to impress upon her. Even a counselor she'd talked to had tried to make her see that it had been a horrible accident. That she hadn't been responsible.

But how could she accept that?

"I talked her into crossing the road. Our parents gave us strict orders to stay on the sidewalk but I wanted to go to the park."

"You were ten at the time."

"I should have known better."

They sat in silence for several minutes. He continued to hold her. She should move. She knew better than to sit in the comfort of his arms, but it felt like a safe haven.

"I'm sure your parents don't blame you," he said softly.

"They do blame me. They always have. And I've spent years trying to make it up to them. I've tried to be the best daughter I could be. I've made every decision based on what would please them. My sister was amazing. She was smart and funny. She wouldn't have crossed that street but she wouldn't allow me to go alone."

"It only seemed that way because you were ten and she was your big sister," he said after a while. "Things happen that change us. What matters is how we move forward. Or don't."

She eased from his warm embrace. "You're speaking from experience?"

He smiled but she wasn't fooled by the gesture. There was no warmth in his eyes. It was a gesture, nothing more.

"I killed my father," he said simply, then got up and moved away from her.

* * *

Alex grabbed the plastic tub that was labeled Ornaments and slid it toward the opening in the floor. Marissa continued to watch him, her expression thoughtful. Of course she would have a ton of questions for him.

"Why do you think that?" she asked.

"I was an angry teenager. He'd abused us. He'd taken advantage of people in the community. I just wanted him gone. And that day, when he got on that bull because he had to show me how it was done, I told him I hoped it took him down. And it did."

"But you didn't kill him."

"No. I didn't. But for a long time, I thought I did."

"We're a mess," she finally said.

He sat down with his back against the container of decorations. "Yeah, I guess. I like to think I'm a survivor. I've been trying to get my head on straight and working on realizing that I didn't write my father's destiny. He made choices. He wasn't a good person. And when he got on that bull, my thoughts didn't control what happened."

"No, they didn't."

He was close enough to touch her, but didn't. "I do control the choices I make and how I deal with the things that have happened in my life.

I'm not perfect. I'm definitely flawed. But I like to think I'm in a better place than I was a few years ago."

For instance, if he'd been a little braver, he would have told her that he was starting to believe he could be the man who wouldn't let her down. She needed someone like that. But he knew better than to say the words.

Sitting there on the dusty wood floor of that attic, even in the light of a single bulb hanging from the ceiling, she looked like someone's princess. Even in jeans, an old denim jacket and her hair framing her face in chunky layers. She didn't look like a woman a cowboy like him should be thinking about.

It was hard to connect this woman who wore Dan's old jacket and did her best to drive his truck to the woman she was in Dallas, before she landed on the side of the road in Bluebonnet.

"We should get these decorations back to the house before Dan comes looking for us," he suggested. Mainly because he needed to get her back before his heart started playing tricks on him. He stood and then reached for her hand.

He knew it was mistake immediately, reaching for her hand. But he held it, pulling her to her feet. Then she was in front of him. He touched her hair, curling the soft strands around his finger. His knuckle brushed her cheek and she closed her eyes.

He took his time as he brushed his lips over hers. Kissing her was a gift. He'd never felt that away about a woman before, as if she should be treasured. This woman made him feel that. And more.

Truth be told, what she really made him feel was scared to death.

He slowly broke contact. She slid her fingers from his.

"Hey. Did you two get lost up there?" Dan yelled from the tack room beneath them.

"No, Dan, just going through all of this stuff you've packed away up here. Who knew you were a hoarder? You should be on a reality show." Alex peeked through the door. "Hey, what do you have in this locked box up here?"

"Stay out of there. That's my retirement."

Marissa was restacking boxes and wouldn't look at him. Alex walked up behind her, smoothed her hair and kissed her cheek.

"I'm sorry," he whispered. "Not for kissing you. But because you've been hurt. I don't want to be another person who hurts you."

"You won't," she said with confidence.

He wished he could believe that.

"I'll carry the decorations to the house. Is there anything else you want from up here?"

"No. I think that's all we need." She reached for the chain on the light but she didn't pull. She stared at him for a few seconds.

"You okay?" he asked.

"I'm good." She managed a smile. "We should go."

He went first, carrying the decorations on his shoulder as he went down the ladder. Almost to the bottom, Dan took it from him. Alex waited for Marissa to climb down. She didn't need his help but he waited, just in case. When she reached the bottom, she grinned.

"Let's go decorate that tree," she said brightly, as if a short time ago she hadn't fallen apart, and as if the kiss had meant nothing.

The sun had come out and the clouds were breaking up, showing patches of blue in the sky. The three of them trudged across the lawn with Bub following along. They were almost to the camper when the dog started howling, the ear-splitting noise piercing the quiet. In response to the dog's warning, the rooster flew across the yard and landed on the porch.

"Car coming," Dan said as they headed up the stairs of the camper. "He does that when he hears unfamiliar tires on the road."

Alex kind of doubted the dog was that smart. But sure enough a car had turned off the main road and was easing down Dan's driveway. Next to him, Marissa drew in a breath and whispered something he couldn't hear.

"Who is it?" he asked.

She stood on the rickety front porch of Dan's camper and with a shake of her head walked back down the steps. "My parents."

They parked next to his truck and sat for a full minute. Alex remained on the porch next to Dan, because he thought Dan might need a friend. But he was torn between Dan and Marissa, who was standing in the yard waiting to greet her parents. He guessed she needed a friend, too.

Not thirty minutes ago she'd felt like a lot more than a friend. She'd felt like the best thing to ever happen to him.

The car doors finally opened and she took a few, hesitant steps forward. He wanted to go to her, to stand next to her. It wasn't his place, to be at her side. These were her parents. He guessed there was a lot of distance between them but they were still her family.

He was just the cowboy who had picked up a bride on the side of the road. She wasn't even his bride.

"Let's go inside and have coffee," Dan said as he turned away from the scene playing out in the yard.

"I should probably head on home."

Dan shook his head but he shot a look back

at Marissa and her family. "I wouldn't go if I was you. She's probably going to want a couple of allies."

Marissa joined her parents as they got out of the car. They were talking quietly, hugging each other. Yeah, Dan had the right of it. She was going to need a couple of allies. To an outsider, it looked like a normal scene, but there was something a bit off.

"You think you might need an ally, too?" he asked Dan.

The older man gave him a sheepish grin. "I might. I taught that woman to ride a horse and drive a tractor. She was a little bitty thing back then. And I also watched her mom load her up in a car and drive her away from here. Guess I'll have to watch another little girl get loaded up in a car and dragged away from this ranch."

"I'm sorry, Dan." Alex patted him on the shoulder. "If it helps, I think even if she leaves today, she'll be back."

"Nice of you to think so. Don't get your hopes up, cowboy." With that, Dan opened the camper door and walked inside.

Alex followed him in but he couldn't help but think that Dan should be involved in the family reunion. After all, it was his daughter and his granddaughter out there. Instead he was fixing himself a cup of coffee as if it didn't matter. As if it had nothing to do with him.

"Stop staring out the window," Dan muttered as he kicked back in the recliner. "Ain't nothing you or me can do about it. She has to make her own decisions. Don't you have enough on your plate without worrying over what she's doing to do?"

The ranch. Alex had to agree. He stepped away from the window and allowed Marissa her privacy because he had creditors nipping at his heels and not a lot of time to solve his own problems.

Chapter Twelve

Marissa hugged her mom and then her dad. It didn't matter that she was an adult or that there was distance between them, they were still her parents and she still wanted their hugs. But in their embrace she still felt like the child they resented, the one who had let them down, the one who hadn't lived up to their dreams.

"I'm sorry," she whispered as her mom hugged her a second time.

"Stop," her mother said, surprising her. "You aren't the one who should apologize. Aidan should have talked to you. He should have had the decency to end things sooner."

"And he shouldn't have hurt you," her father said. "I can't imagine how any man would walk out on you."

It took a minute for the words to sink in.

The words were healing. Her parents were

here for her. She swiped at the tears that rolled down her cheeks. Her mom brushed a hand against the dampness, then her fingers sifted through the strands of her now shoulder-length hair.

"Don't ever become a beautician."

"Don't worry. I realize I have no skills in that department," Marissa assured her. "I have found I'm decent with a tractor and I'm something of a rooster whisperer."

"Also not skills I'd want to encourage."

Her mom froze, as if suddenly realizing where she was. She glanced around. "It's been so long. I'd almost forgotten this place."

"Come inside." Marissa took her by the hand.

"I'm not sure if I want to."

Marissa's dad moved to her mother's side. Marissa had seen it all of her life but had somehow missed it. Her parents supported each other. They leaned on one another. She should have wanted that in her relationship with Aidan. Instead she'd only ever thought of him as an escape route. She'd wanted someone—anyone—to be her person. And she hadn't allowed herself to really see what they had, which had been less than friendship.

"We really just came to take you home," her mother assured her.

Back to Dallas. Marissa glanced from her

parents to the camper. "I'm not quite ready yet. There's a potluck at church. And a Christmas program. I'd like to be here for those things."

"This isn't your home," her mother insisted.

"No, it isn't. But I have family here. I have a grandfather. We were getting ready to decorate his Christmas tree. I think he hasn't had one in a while."

A family or a tree.

"Marissa, please." Her mom reached for her but her hand dropped short of contact. "We want you to come home."

"I will. I promise. But I need to be here right now. Why don't you come inside, just for a minute? There's coffee." She looked from her father to her mother. She called on all of that backbone that had gotten her through life. "And there's a man in there who is your father."

Her mom drew in a deep breath, then she nodded. "Okay, a cup of coffee and then we have to go. But you'll come home before Christmas?"

"I'll come home before Christmas."

They walked up the steps of the camper and she opened the door, now more nervous than she had thought she'd be. Alex was inside with her grandfather. What would her parents think of the man who had picked her up on the side of the road?

The three of them made the cramped confines

of the camper seem even smaller. Marissa took her mom by the hand. She led her the few feet to where Dan sat in his recliner watching them, his eyes misty as he pretended to sip his coffee.

"It hasn't changed much," he said gruffly. "But I guess I have. You certainly have. It's good to see you, Mary."

Then he waited, and Marissa knew his heart would break if her mother turned away from him. She knew, because on the day Lisa had died, her mom had turned away from her. She'd closed herself off and she hadn't realized that Marissa's heart was breaking, too.

For a long time Marissa thought it would always be that way, that they would exist in this world separately. They would look like a family, do the things families did, but there would be invisible walls.

Dan put the footstool of the recliner down and pushed himself to his feet. He stood there looking down at his daughter, now a grown woman.

"You look a lot like your mother," he said. "And I've missed you every single day for these forty odd years. Every day. Your mom sent me pictures and occasionally we talked."

"She talked to you?" Marissa's mom shook her head. "I thought we left and never looked back."

He scratched his chin. "I guess in a way you did. But your mom and I, we talked. You know, we never got a divorce. I always kind of thought she'd come back eventually. Maybe she'd get you raised and remember she had a husband."

"I'm so sorry," Mary said. "I didn't know."

Marissa caught movement out of the corner of her eye. She glanced back as Alex headed for the door, pushing his hat down on his head as he went.

"Don't you dare leave," she ordered. "We have a tree to decorate and pies to make."

He paused at the door. Face shadowed by the brim of the hat, he looked from her mom to her dad and back to her. "I should go."

No, he shouldn't. She wanted him there. No, she *needed* him. And she had never really needed anyone. No, that wasn't true. She'd needed her parents.

"We're going to decorate the tree," she reminded him. The tree was important to her. It was her way of belonging here, in her grandfather's life.

"Oh, sit back down, Alex. It isn't like they'll stay long." Her grandfather had moved to the kitchen and he was pouring another cup of coffee. "Here, have a cup."

He held the cup out to Alex. "Mary and what's your name? Joe? This is my neighbor, Alex Palermo. He helps me out from time to time."

Marissa's dad stepped forward to shake Alex's

hand. "Good to meet you, Alex. I'm Joe Walker. And thank you. For everything."

For rescuing his daughter off the side of the road, he meant. Her mom looked uncomfortable, her attention focusing on the floor and not the people around her. She finally lifted her gaze to meet Alex's.

"We are glad to meet you." She looked at her watch. "But we really should go now. Marissa, do you want to get your stuff?"

Marissa should have expected that. Her parents had shown up with a purpose. To take her home. And they weren't taking no for an answer. "Mom, I just told you. I'm not going. Not yet. I'll be home in time for Christmas. And I plan on starting my job in January. But I need to stay here a little longer."

Her mom's eyes widened and she looked past Marissa to Dan. And to Alex. "You're staying *here*?"

Mary Walker glanced around the tiny camper. Her gaze landed on Bub, the bloodhound. The dog picked that moment to stretch and yawn. Marissa chuckled at the dog, because he really didn't care who had come to visit.

"I see," her mom finally said.

"Stay and help us decorate the tree?" Marissa invited.

Her mom looked from Bub to the tiny tree

in front of the window. "No, we should go. It's a long drive back. We have plans this evening. Will you walk us out?"

"Of course." Marissa glanced at her grandfather, coffee still in hand.

"Well, I guess I'll be seeing you around." He said it with a casual tone, as if they were neighbors who had met up at the local café.

Marissa watched her mother's expression change, soften. She stepped forward to hug Dan. "Yes, we'll be back."

Dan patted her on the back, awkwardly, with the cup of coffee. Alex stepped forward and took the cup from his hand.

"Mary, you've done well. And this little girl is one to be proud of." He leaned close. "Don't live in the past. Time to live the life you've got."

Marissa's mom brushed at tears and nodded. "Thank you, Dan. Dad." She laughed a little. "Thank you."

She hurried out the door and Marissa followed. When they reached the car, Marissa's mom stopped. She ran a shaking hand down her face, and, with tears still shimmering in her eyes, she hugged Marissa tight.

"Don't fall in love with a cowboy. Let your heart heal and come home to figure out what you'll do next."

Marissa laughed at the advice. "I'm not going

to fall in love with a cowboy and I will be home. I take that back. I have fallen in love with a cowboy. He's my grandfather. He's gruff and says what he thinks, but I do love him."

Mary nodded as she let go of Marissa's hands and moved toward the car. "Yes, and he loves you, too."

"Daddy, goodbye." She hurried to give her father a hug. "I'll call and you'll come get me?"

"I'll come get you no matter where you are."

She watched her parents drive back down the dusty dirt driveway. When she turned to go back inside, Alex was there. He waited for her at the porch, concern narrowing his eyes as he looked from her to the car in the distance.

"You're okay?" he asked.

"I'm good. Really, probably better than I've been in years. And I just bought myself a little more time in Bluebonnet."

His smile faded. "I'm glad. Dan is less cantankerous with you here."

"I'm not sure about that," she answered. "I know I'll have to go back eventually. I have a job and responsibilities."

"Of course."

"We should decorate the tree and make those pies." She looped her arm through his and together they walked back inside. "But I insist on knowing the recipe."

"I'm not about to tell you how I make my pies. What kind of woman are you, going after a man's secrets?"

She pulled him close. "I want all of your secrets."

"There are some things you just can't have, Marissa Walker. And my secret pie recipe is one of them."

She could have corrected him. She wanted his secrets, not his pie recipe. She wanted more time with him, too.

But she guessed he was right about this: there were some things she couldn't have.

The camper smelled of apples and cinnamon. Alex opened the tub of ornaments while Marissa wrapped the little tree in lights. He guessed he shouldn't poke fun at their tree. He'd bought one for his house that came already decorated.

"That pie sure smells good," Dan said from his chair.

He'd watched as they made the pies. The process had taken longer than usual because Marissa hadn't been much of a hand peeling and slicing apples. And she'd kept trying to watch as he measured out the ingredients to mix with the apples. He'd moved to block her view and she'd tried to put her hands on his shoulders and peek around him.

"Do I get a piece of that pie tonight?" Dan asked as he got up to mess with his old portable record player he'd pulled out of the closet. Soon Bing Crosby was singing Christmas songs.

"You stay out of the pie, Dan." Alex picked a small box of ornaments. When he opened it, it was like opening a time vault.

Marissa plugged in the lights and the tree lit up. He had to admit, lights made it better. He handed her the box of ornaments. She sifted through the homemade decorations, most of which had her mother's name on them. Who would have guessed Dan to be sentimental? Not in all of the years Alex had known him had he thought Dan cared about anything other than this piece of land he had and the bloodhound that emitted more noxious odors than a defective septic tank.

"Don't start thinking I'm sappy or something," Dan said as he hooked himself up to his oxygen. "I'm cheap. That's all. When my wife left she took what mattered. She took Mary. She left the rest for me. The camper. The bills. The ornaments. A few pictures."

"Of course, and you kept them all." Marissa pulled out a star made with yarn wrapped around sticks. And then a glitter-covered manger scene. She handed Alex back the box and she started to hang decorations. He didn't say anything, just watched as she placed the decorations on branches that sagged a bit from the weight.

After she'd finished with the homemade ornaments, she moved onto old bulbs that were brightly painted but chipped and faded in spots. She hung each and every one of those decorations. When she finished she stepped back and the tree had been transformed, thanks to glitter and twinkling lights. The red bulbs that had originally been hung twinkled amongst the older decorations.

"Not bad," Dan said. "That's not bad at all. Now why don't the two of you head to town for dinner? I'm going to take a nap but you can bring me back a cheeseburger."

Alex glanced at his watch. "I'd love to do that but I've got a meeting at the church."

"You aren't becoming your dad, are you? That's the last thing this town needs, another Palermo fleecing the flock."

Alex somehow managed a tight smile. "No, Dan, I'm not Jesse Palermo. And you know Pastor Matthews is nothing like my father."

"I know but I'm just making sure. I wouldn't want you caught up in something you couldn't get out of."

"I'm not. I'm going to the church to help Lucy with her self-defense class."

"What are you going to do at a self-defense class?" Curiosity gleamed in Dan's eyes.

"Oh, you'd be surprised," Alex answered without really answering. He knew if he gave too many details, he'd never hear the end of it.

"So you're not going to tell me…" Dan paused and finally shrugged. "How's those bucking bulls and the tractor repair?"

"I guess I won't starve," Alex answered as he headed for the kitchen and the pies. He didn't add that he had bigger concerns. But since Dan had seen the foreclosure notice in the paper, he guessed it wasn't a secret.

"Is Marcus not willing to help you out?" Dan asked, his tone suggesting he was truly concerned.

Alex shrugged. "I'm not sure he wants to keep the place. I'm going to get a loan or sell off cattle. It'll work out."

"Cattle prices are down." Dan cleared his throat. "Drought makes people nervous, even though we've been getting rain. But you're right, it'll work out. If they have something to eat at the church, would you bring me back some supper?"

Marissa shot her grandfather a warning look. "I'm making pasta and salad."

"Green stuff." Dan made a face and waved them away. "Go on, then. I guess we'll see you at church tomorrow. Green food and Jesus. She's taking over my life."

"I guess I could take her off your hands." Alex winked at Marissa. "For the right price. I'll even bring you back a few tacos from the dinner they're serving at church."

"You take her off my hands and I'll double your wages for helping out around here." Dan cackled as he made the offer.

"Dan, double of nothing is still nothing. And even if I take her, I bet she'll still make you eat some vegetables with those tacos."

"For a few hours of peace and quiet, it'll be worth it. Sometimes a man just wants to nap and watch a car race without a woman squawking that there's a good movie she's missing."

"She might not want to go." Alex chanced a look at the woman in question. She was standing quietly, looking at the tree.

"*She* might have an opinion of her own," Marissa answered at long last.

"Marissa, would you like to go to town with me?"

Her hand dropped from the ornament she'd been touching. It was a horse made of baked dough and on the back her mother had written "I love you, Daddy."

He wondered about a family that had mementos that spoke of love, and yet they'd been split apart at the seams and never put back together.

Dan noticed what had caught her attention. "She was horse-crazy, your mom was. She had this little spotted pony she'd ride around on. She said she was a rodeo queen."

"That must be why she always sent me to a summer camp with horses. Every summer."

"I'm glad she did that for you," Dan said in a gruff tone that might have meant he didn't care. Alex knew he cared a lot.

"So am I." Marissa grabbed her jacket off the hook by the door. "Are we going?"

Alex glanced back at Dan. The older man was pretending he no longer cared. "Yes, we're going."

"Okay, but this isn't a date."

"Definitely not a date," he assured her.

Dan flipped on the TV. "Would the two of you just go? And don't be a cheap date, Alex. You can't keep a woman if you're cheap. That's why you're twenty-seven and still single. You're cheap."

"Dan, you're knocking on the door of eighty and you're single."

"And I was cheap," he grumbled and turned up the volume on the TV. "Go on now. Have her home at a decent hour and don't go down any back roads."

"Thanks, Granddad. I feel like I'm sixteen and going to the prom."

"Well, I missed out on a lot. I have to make up for all of those little moments." He tapped his cheek but he didn't smile. Marissa understood and hurried to his side to kiss his cheek.

"You're a mess."

"Yes, I am. Be careful. Don't fall for a cowboy. All lines, but no follow-through."

Alex opened the front door for the woman who wasn't his date, but he leaned back in to tell Dan goodbye. "And for your information, I don't have lines. Or follow-through."

"You're the worst kind," Dan called out as the door closed.

Alex led Marissa across the yard to his truck. He opened the door for her and helped her in. Was it just a few weeks ago that she'd appeared in his life? It seemed as if he'd known her forever.

Chapter Thirteen

Alex stood in front of Lucy in the church fellowship hall. The women from the shelter and a few ladies from the community usually attended the self-defense classes. Today Marissa stood amongst the women. He tried to avoid looking her way but that was easier said than done.

Occasionally his gaze strayed, the same way his thoughts strayed. She wouldn't be here much longer. He guessed that was probably for the best. Since she'd shown up, he'd been distracted. He'd managed to get his own work done but he'd also spent a lot more time at Dan's than he normally would have.

Vaguely he heard Lucy tell him to come at her from behind. She said something to the crowd of women that made them all giggle. He put his hands up and before he could prepare, Lucy had him by the arm and flying through the air. His back hit the floor.

He groaned and tried to take a breath. Lucy looked down, grinning at him. "That's what you get for being distracted. Ladies, being aware of your surroundings will help to keep you safe. As you can see from my brother's position, flat on his back, being distracted is dangerous."

"Find yourself a new victim," he groaned as he sat up.

"Oh, but that's where you're mistaken. We are not victims. We are empowered because we know how to protect ourselves. And you are not the victim, you're the attacker."

He sat for a minute with his arms resting across his bent knees. "Yeah, well, you seemed to have forgotten that I'm not really attacking you."

"When did you get so soft?" she asked.

"I'm not soft."

She held a hand out and pulled him to his feet.

"Let's go over some basics. If you're in a parking lot, walking down the street or even in your own home, do you know what to do? I want you to remember, it is always better to fight, to call attention to yourself and to run. If you go with an attacker, your odds of escape decrease." Lucy positioned him in the center of the mat.

Alex made his best scared face to get a giggle

out of the women watching the demonstration. Many of them had escaped abusive relationships, and smiling was something they didn't do a lot of. Not yet. The hope was that as time went on, they would smile more.

No one understood that better than Alex and Lucy. Lucy had left home at eighteen, intent on escaping the abusive home they'd grown up in. Alex had done his best to stay on the edge of his father's radar. He'd gained the most attention when he tried to protect his siblings, or distract their father.

He hadn't always been successful.

Lucy snapped her fingers to get his attention. "Cowboy up and pay attention, Alex. What has you so distracted tonight?"

Heat crawled up his neck. "Just tell me what you want me to do."

"Come at me from the front."

He did his best, knowing he wouldn't win. No one went up against Lucy and won. She was trained in hand-to-hand combat. She was a bodyguard and she'd been an MP in the army. She could outshoot, outrun and outfight him. He was okay with that. She would never again be anyone's victim.

Lucy explained that even if a woman had her hands blocked or the attacker held her, she still had a foot, a knee, a head. Alex raised his hands and backed away. Lucy grinned at his cowardice.

"Come on, Alex, come at me."

"I think I'm done."

She motioned him on, so he moved to grab her. She showed the women a variety of techniques to block his attempts and also to bring him to his knees.

"Lucy Palermo, that isn't nice," Bea said. He gave her a quick grin as Aunt Essie tried to quiet her. "I sure don't think she should hit her brother that way."

"It's okay, Bea, she won't hurt me." Alex stepped away from his sister. "She wants to show you how to defend yourself if anyone ever tries to hurt you."

Bea's face took on a soft, kind of sad look. Alex didn't know what to do or say when she started to cry. He walked off the mat and gathered the older woman in a hug.

"Bea, did someone hurt you?"

She leaned against him, sobbing until she hiccupped. "Yes, and it wasn't neighborly."

"No, Bea, it probably wasn't. I'm sorry." Alex gave his aunt an imploring look because tears were not part of his job description.

Bea didn't seem to care. "I had a baby, Alex. She was a pretty little girl and they took her away and said I wasn't able to raise her. I heard the nurse say I wasn't in my right mind. But I was."

"Honey, let's go home now." Essie took Bea by the hand. "We'll work on self-defense another day."

"But I wanted to help decorate for the Christmas program." Bea wiped away her tears.

Out of the corner of his eye, Alex saw Marissa leave with a couple of the women from the shelter. He'd catch up with her later. At the moment, Essie more than likely needed his help with Bea.

"Bea, would you like to help me put the finishing touches on the manger that we've set up on the stage. It needs some shingles on the roof. If you're good with a hammer."

"I am good with a hammer." Bea smiled brightly, stories of neighbors and babies forgotten. But he wouldn't forget. Somewhere out there, Bea had a little girl.

"Let's go hammer then." He led her through the church to the sanctuary.

Pastor Matthews and a couple of men from the church were working on the stable that would be the center for any nativity dramas performed at the Christmas program. One of the men stood on a ladder attaching a star to the highest peak of the ceiling.

Alex spotted Marissa sitting on the piano bench. Her hands began to move across the keys and he stopped to listen as she played "Silent Night." The women she'd been talking to now sat on a nearby pew listening. She played the piano. He guessed he shouldn't be surprised.

She could ride a horse, drive Dan's tractor and play the piano. If he had to guess, he thought she could probably do anything she set her mind to. He guessed she did whatever she thought would make her parents happy. With one exception.

She'd stayed in Bluebonnet. For Dan.

As his mind had wandered, he'd lost Bea. She had moved to the piano bench and was in the process of scooting Marissa over so that she could sit next to her.

Marissa glanced at the other woman and gave her a sweet smile, but kept playing. They were quite a pair, Marissa in her blue jeans and over-size flannel shirt; Bea in her floral house dress, still wearing her hairnet from work. But Bea's feet were bouncing in time to the music and, without warning, she started singing the chorus of "Silent Night."

She blew the roof off that little old church with the sweetest rendition of that song Alex had ever heard. From the looks of things, the music was having a similar effect on everyone. The hammers stopped. Pastor Matthews and the men sat down. The ladies stood silently in the background. Bea and Marissa entered a world of their own.

Alex desperately wanted to be in that world with them, because from the expressions on their faces, it was a good place to be.

As "Silent Night" ended, it became clear that Bea was on a roll. She flipped the pages to another song. Marissa nodded and began to play. This time she joined Bea and the two of them sang "Carol of the Bells." It was clear that Bea was directing things. She would sing and occasionally point at the music and Marissa would chime in.

When they finished, Bea turned red and hung her head. Emotion hung heavy in the air and no one spoke. They were all too stunned. Alex sat back, watching as Marissa hugged the other woman tight and told her something that encouraged her to smile and look up. Marissa took her hand and stood with her. That's when everyone stood and applauded the duo.

Alex's gaze connected with Marissa's and he was almost knocked over from the strength of emotion that stretched between them. It was more than the song. He tried to tell himself it was the moment or the music, but he knew better. And he knew he had to do something to break this connection.

He walked away—he'd think up an excuse later.

* * *

Marissa knew a person couldn't really forget how to breathe but that's how she felt when she looked up and met Alex's gaze. His dark eyes had been full of emotion. And then he'd simply turned and walked away.

It hurt that he would walk away from her. She got that it didn't make sense, this imagined connection between the two of them. She shouldn't give it more credence than it deserved. She had always dealt in hard facts. She had managed for a very long time to keep her emotions in firm check. For her sake. For her mother's.

Stop crying, her mother had told her all of those years ago. *Just stop*. She couldn't undo what had happened with tears. She couldn't make it all okay again.

But she'd tried. She'd tried so hard. With every tear she blinked away. With every test she aced. With every award she earned. She had tried.

What had it gotten her?

Lonely. It had gotten her loneliness. It had brought her to the doorstep of a grandfather she hadn't known existed and into the life of a man who didn't want to be troubled by her.

Further thoughts were interrupted by the approach of Pastor Matthews. He looked from Marissa to Bea and back before shaking his head and grinning. She didn't know what to say to that, because she had been just as astounded by Bea's voice.

"That was amazing. Will the two of you perform for the Christmas program?"

The invitation took her by surprise. She glanced past him to Alex, who had taken up a hammer and was helping the men put shingles on the makeshift stable. Someone plugged in the cord attached to the star and it lit up, glowing bright with Christmas lights.

Alex shifted just a bit, his dark eyes boring into her. She shook off the lingering feelings of losing something important.

Next to her, Bea didn't hesitate. "We would love to, Preacher. I do love to sing. Mama always told me not to go around town bragging about my singing. She said it was a sin. That's what Pastor Palermo told her. She sure liked the pastor. But I like you better." She glanced at Alex. "I'm sorry about that, Alex."

"I'm not sure if I'll be here," Marissa answered when Pastor Matthews directed his attention to her.

"But you have to," Bea interjected. She gave Marissa and then Alex a reproachful look before leaning toward Pastor Matthews. "Alex has been neighborly and my mama said that's a sin."

"Being neighborly is a sin, Bea? How is that?" Pastor Matthews looked truly confused.

"Don't. Ask," Alex shouted, getting everyone's attention. He swung the hammer at a nail and then jerked his hand back. "Ouch."

"That's what a temper will get you Alex Palermo." Bea shook her head. "He needs to repent. He also needs to repent because he looks at Marissa like he wants to kiss her."

"Bea, I think it's about time I take you home." Aunt Essie to the rescue.

Bea grumbled as she grabbed her enormous purse and swung it over her shoulder. "You're the one who said it, Essie. You told Libby that Alex is in big trouble and he can't look at—"

"Stop," Essie whispered a little too loudly.

Marissa was stuck somewhere between humor and wanting the floor to open and swallow her up. Essie offered a sheepish smile.

"I'm going to take Bea home. But I do hope you can be here for the Christmas program, Marissa. That music was beautiful."

"Thank you," she answered. Turning to Bea, she said, "Bea, I'm not sure how a beautiful voice like yours could ever be a sin and I hope you sing often."

"And I concur," Pastor Matthews added.

Bea gave him a narrow-eyed look. "If I wasn't getting in trouble by Miss Essie, I'd ask what *concur* means."

"It means I agree, Bea. Having your beautiful

voice and singing those songs for God is not a sin." Pastor Matthews hugged Bea. "I'm looking forward to hearing you sing more."

Marissa excused herself and went in search of Alex. He was no longer working on the stable. The other men were packing up tools and the star had been unplugged. She walked through the church and didn't find him anywhere. She wondered if he might have left, forgetting that she needed a ride. Or maybe not caring.

He hadn't left her, though. She found him outside, a short distance from the church, sitting on a bench near the playground. As she approached, he looked up, unsmiling.

"I'm sorry." She didn't know what else to say.

"For what?"

She sat down next to him. "I'm not sure. It would help if *you* would tell *me* what I'm apologizing for."

One side of his mouth tugged upward, easing the tension in his expression. "I'm not mad at you, so you don't have to apologize."

"Bea?"

He shook his head. "No, I would never be angry with Bea. She says whatever is on her mind. She can't help that. I'm angry because my father told her she shouldn't sing. That voice, tonight when she sang and you played, that was amazing. It made me feel maybe a little bit of the awe those shepherds felt when they approached the stable, knowing they'd find their savior inside."

He managed to put into words what she'd felt sitting next to Bea. As she'd played, the men had ceased working on the stable, but one of them had continued to work on the star. The lights would twinkle and go out and they would try again. It had brought that long-ago night to life in her imagination. Silent night, holy night.

"A gift like Bea's shouldn't be wasted," Alex said. "But my father, for whatever reason, had tried to silence that voice. Maybe because of what happened to Bea. Or he might have been jealous. Logic never mattered to Jesse Palermo."

"I'm sorry." Somehow his hand ended up in hers.

"Thank you." He gave her hand a light squeeze. "We should go. Pastor Matthews would be upset if he thought we were being neighborly in front of the church."

She giggled. "Bea does have a way with words."

"Yes, she does." He stood, still holding her hand, and led her to his truck.

The night was cool and crystal clear with millions of stars twinkling overhead in the inky darkness of the sky. The world seemed so much bigger here, with no buildings to mar the skyline, no lights to compete with the brightness of the moon or the stars. She'd always thought the city, with all of the people, the cars, the buildings, was big. But this quiet, country night changed that for her.

When a person could stand in the yard and see the sun come up in the east, the colors as brilliant as spilled paint across the morning sky, and then in the evening watch the sun set on the opposite horizon, there was a hugeness in that.

She drew in a deep breath of the cold December air, closing her eyes as she waited for Alex to unlock and open the truck door.

"There's nothing like this air," she told him.

"No, there isn't. And a night like this, when the moon is that bright."

She looked up, nodding her agreement. "It almost looks as if you could reach out and touch it."

"Yes, it does."

She became aware of the man standing in front of her. His hand was touching her cheek and there was a sweetness in his expression.

"Bea would be appalled," he whispered. "But I'm about to kiss you."

"We shouldn't."

"Yeah, I've never been the best at should and shouldn't."

He kissed her as his fingers stroked a sweet line along her jaw. The kiss was everything. It made her feel treasured and beautiful. It made her feel like the woman she wanted to be. His woman.

No. She wasn't his. She didn't know how to trust what she felt, not after Aidan. She had tried to be who Aidan wanted her to be, too. She'd tried to fit into his world. The same way she'd always tried to please her parents, she realized. And here she was, feeding chickens and driving a tractor.

Kissing a cowboy and wanting to be the person who fit in his life.

The sounds of people talking and laughing, a car starting, helped to bring her back to reality. She moved a step back from Alex, and from emotions that were jumbled up.

It made sense that they shouldn't talk just yet, so she was glad when wordlessly he opened the door for her. She climbed inside the warm, confining space of the truck cab. Alex got in and started to speak.

"I'm going to miss you."

She would miss him, too. "I'll be back from time to time."

"Right. Of course."

That wasn't the answer he wanted but she didn't know what else to say. The kiss had been a revelation. It had also revealed some things about her life and how she'd been living it. Pleasing others, trying to be who they wanted her to be.

She had obligations, responsibilities, back in Dallas. Most of all she knew that it was time for her to figure out what she really wanted out of life and who she really wanted to be.

Chapter Fourteen

Marissa bit back the grin she knew her grandfather wouldn't appreciate. He was sitting next to her in the church pew wearing his Sunday best, which happened to be new bib overalls and a button-up shirt with his good boots.

"Church," he grumbled. "I can't believe I let you talk me into going to church."

"It isn't going to hurt you," she said calmly.

"You don't know that it isn't. And don't sass me."

"I'm not sassing, I'm telling you that this won't hurt you."

A few rows of ahead of them, Alex sat with his family. Aunt Essie, his sister Lucy and her husband, Dane, and his younger sister, Maria. Alex glanced back at them, teeth flashing as he grinned. Next to him, Essie gave him a pointed look. A warning, if Marissa had to guess.

The warnings should have come sooner. Someone should have warned Marissa that a too-charming cowboy with funny ears would make it difficult for her to leave Bluebonnet Springs behind. Even when she knew she did have to go. She'd signed a contract for a teaching position. She wasn't the country girl she'd been pretending to be.

"Stop looking at the boy that way. People are going to wonder." Her grandfather spoke in a too-loud whisper, and the people around them giggled.

"Shh," Marissa warned her grandfather.

He chuckled as if it happened to be great fun. Her heart filled up. With love for him, for this town and for a God who was as real to her today as He had been all of those years ago when she'd been a child in Sunday school.

The service started. She'd never been so thankful for anything. She could sit there in relative peace, sing songs she hadn't forgotten, listen to a message of hope and stare at the back of Alex's head.

The service ended and people started making their way to the fellowship hall. Dan and Marissa joined the crowd, somehow falling in with Alex and his family as they made their way down the short hallway to the kitchen area.

"That wasn't so bad, was it, Dan?" Alex asked

as they entered the big, fluorescent-lit room with the many tables and chairs set up with pretty evergreen centerpieces.

"No, not bad at all." But he pulled on his collar and shivered. "There sure are a bunch of people here."

Marissa took her took her grandfather by the hand. "Yes, there are. And you need to sit down."

He bristled a bit. "I think I know when I need to sit down."

"Of course you do." She paused and waited.

"Now I need to sit down." His blue eyes twinkled. "I just like to decide these things for myself."

Essie walked past. "Dan, you look pretty spiffy today."

"Charm me all you want, Essie, you're not getting my money."

"You might smell kind of good, but you don't have that much money."

He took a seat and looked around. "Now what is the plan? I thought you were going to feed us."

"We have to get the food set out and then we'll start a line," Essie informed him with a pat on his shoulder. "You won't be sorry, Dan."

"I know I won't."

"What can I do to help?" Marissa asked as Essie started to hurry off.

Essie glanced toward the kitchen and then

looked around. "I don't really know. There are already too many women in the kitchen. There are some smaller children that are starting to look restless. Would you corral them while their mothers finish getting the food ready?"

Children, she knew how to handle. "Of course. Can I take them outside?"

Essie lifted a shoulder. "Suits me. In the closet by the door there are bubbles, balls and other outdoor toys."

Alex had disappeared. He'd mentioned helping the pastor put something in the attic. Marissa wouldn't wait for him. She could handle a few children on her own. She gathered up the kids, who seemed restless, and headed them out the door, stopping on her way to get bubbles, Frisbees and a ball.

"What are we going to do?" Amy, the little girl she'd met on her previous trips to the church, asked.

"Whatever you want, as long as it is safe." Marissa led them to the playground and she laid out the items she'd procured from the closet. "What do you all want to do?"

"Tag!" one of the boys yelled.

A chant of, "Tag, tag!" went up from the group of half a dozen children.

"Okay, tag it is. Who is going to be 'it' first?"

The biggest boy touched her arm. "You're 'it.'"

That didn't seem fair. But before she could protest, they ran, scattering across the lawn. She chased after one of the bigger boys but he quickly outran her. She went after another and he laughed as he slid past her and kept going. She could see that this wasn't going to go very well for her. If she had any hope of catching any of them, it was one of the little girls. They'd managed to get farther away as the boys kept Marissa distracted.

She went after little Julie. The dark-haired child was laughing and running backward. "Not too close to the parking lot," Marissa called out.

The little girl stopped for a moment, laughing a real belly laugh. A truck suddenly pulled into the parking lot.

"Stay where you're at until the truck stops," Marissa warned.

The little girl peered around the cars to see the truck, then she screamed. Marissa ran forward. Had a bee or a wasp stung her?

"What's wrong?" she asked as she knelt in front of the child. She noticed the other children had congregated at the picnic table and were blowing bubbles.

"My daddy," she whispered through her tears. "I have to go. He can't be here." And then the child ran off.

Marissa stood up. When she turned around,

someone caught her from behind. "Go inside," she screamed.

The children all ran away.

"I'm just here to get my kid." The man held her tight and she heard the flick as he moved his hand. A knife. He had a knife.

"I'm sorry," she said quietly. "I'm new to the area. I didn't know which child was yours."

"I think you did. And I think you're going to help me get her back. You're going to keep walking toward the church. Nice and steady. You're going to tell my wife to hand over my daughter and then you're going to walk me back to the truck."

"They won't give her to you."

"That's why my day got a little better when you showed up," he told her. His breath smelled of onions. His clothes were dirty. She was aware of the rough stubble of his unshaven face as he leaned close.

She wanted away from him. First she wanted the children safe. The older ones had herded the younger children inside. Pastor Matthews stepped outside, Alex and a few other men close behind him.

For some reason she thought about the food getting cold. She laughed at the thought.

"Are you crazy?" the man holding her tightly against his body asked. She felt the knife thump against her arm. She tried to move and he dug it into her forearm. The sting of pain across her arm took her by surprise.

Why had she thought he wouldn't really hurt her? But he wasn't playing. This wasn't a game to him.

As she contemplated her next move, she saw that a woman had joined the men. Lucy.

Seeing the other woman brought back the previous evening's lesson. She focused on Alex's sister and Lucy nodded, as if she knew.

Blood was dripping down Marissa's arm. She tried to move, testing just how he was holding her. He squeezed her wrist and yanked it behind her back.

"Don't try anything funny."

"What would I try? I'm a teacher. It isn't like I'm armed. You have the knife. And I have the cut to prove it."

Get mad, Lucy had said the previous evening. Get mad but don't lose focus. Don't get stupid. Always have a plan. It's one thing they do in their protection business, Lucy had told the ladies. They always knew were the exits were located. They always had an exit plan.

Julie's dad stopped walking. He twisted her arm until she felt her wrist twist. Exit strategy. She couldn't use that arm to hit him. He had a knife. She'd taken a drama class in college.

"I think I'm going to faint."

"Don't you dare," he warned. "Stand up straight."

"I can't." She took a deep breath. "My arm, the blood."

She went limp, hoping beyond hope that it was the right move and praying God had a moment to spare. As she went down it seemed to throw him off balance. He struggled to hold her dead weight and the knife. She took her opportunity and drew her arm back and into his nose, then she knocked him under the chin with her head. He reached for her but she slid to the side and ran.

Alex caught her up against him. "Shh, you're okay. Calm down."

"I can't," she sobbed against him. "I can't be calm now."

"Good job," Lucy said, appearing at her side. "Let's get that arm cleaned up."

"Did he leave?"

"Pastor Matthews is talking to him. The police are on their way."

"Julie and her mom?" Marissa asked as she leaned against Alex.

"Both safe." Lucy nodded at her brother. Without warning he scooped up Marissa in his arms and carried her inside.

"People should go ahead and eat," she told

Lucy as they hurried through the fellowship hall. "And tell my grandfather that I'm fine. It's just a scratch."

"Lucy will tell him. And stop talking." Alex sounded gruff. And angry.

"Why are you mad?" she whispered against his shoulder.

They were in a hallway and he headed for the living area at the back of the shelter.

"You have to ask?"

She did have to ask. And she should also tell him that she could walk just fine. Her arm had been cut, not her legs.

She should have told him to put her down. But she didn't. Because his arms felt strong and safe.

Alex held Marissa a little closer. He could hear the sirens in the distance. He knew how sirens affected her. He also knew that she didn't have a clue how deep the gash on her arm was, or she wouldn't have been so nonchalant about serving lunch.

She'd asked him why he was angry. He was angry because he'd been helping Pastor Matthews and she'd been outside. He hadn't been there. If he'd been with her, he could have kept her safe. As it was, he'd been unable to do anything. He'd had to stand there while that idiot sliced her arm. He'd watched as she went limp and fought to get away.

He'd been pretty proud of her and he guessed it had something to do with Lucy's self-defense class.

Marissa had rescued herself.

He carried her through the door of the family room of the shelter and placed her on the day-bed. Marissa curled up on her side, grimacing as she tried to reach for her arm. It was then that he realized Lucy had followed. She put a towel against the wound and held it tight.

"Doc is getting his bag out of the car. He'll be here in a minute," Lucy said softly. "Marissa, are you feeling okay?"

Marissa opened her eyes. "By okay, do you mean horrible?"

Lucy laughed. "I was hoping for better, but I'll take it."

"I didn't realize how bad it hurt until just now."

Alex stepped away for a moment. He needed to take a deep breath and get control of his temper. Lucy shot him a look over her shoulder. "Get a grip, bro."

"I'm not twelve."

"Children," Marissa said in a whisper. "I'll call the principal."

"I should have been there," Alex said as he scooted a chair close to the bed. "I'm sorry."

"When did you become responsible for me? Or for keeping the whole world safe?" Marissa asked, her eyes a little hazy as she looked down at her arm and then at the wrist that was swelling.

"He's always had this complex," Lucy revealed. And she really shouldn't have. "He wants to keep everyone safe. But even the best of us can't always be there to stop tragedy."

"If I'd been there…" he began.

His sister gave him that scathing look she had. "Stop. If you'd been there, you could have what? Gotten hurt, too? Stopped our dad from locking me up? Stopped the bull from barreling down on one of your best friends?"

"There's nothing wrong with wanting to protect the people you care about."

Marissa lifted her head a few inches. "I'm so glad you care, but really, I did this. I also took care of myself. So stop. You did rescue me off the side of the road. That doesn't mean you took me home to raise."

"You're already raised." The tension drained from his body. "And I'm glad you're okay."

"How's our patient?" Doc hurried through the door. "Looks like she's going to be fine. That's a dandy of a cut, though."

"Did they get him?" Alex asked.

"Still trying to talk to him."

"Is everyone eating lunch?" Marissa asked as Doc pulled the towel off the cut. She grimaced, closing her eyes as he poked around at the wound.

"They're eating. At least it's a good clean cut. I'll have to sew it up. You're not going to like this part. I'm going to give you some shots to deaden that and then…"

"Here? Now?" she asked, her eyes opened wide.

"Unless you want to drive down to my office. I'm not like those fine doctors in Dallas. I take my office with me."

"But stitches?"

Alex pulled another chair close. "He's the best."

"You're going to have to sing to me," Marissa said with a teasing glint in her eyes.

"Sing to her, Doc," Alex said.

"I think she meant for you to sing, Alex." Doc pulled a needle and a small vial out of his bag. "We're going to numb you up a bit. Just be glad this isn't the old days and I'm not giving you a stick to bite."

"Thanks. I think." She closed her eyes again. "Sing, Palermo."

"Silent night, holy night…"

"Stop," she whispered as the needle entered her arm.

"Stop?"

"You're horrible."

Doc laughed. "The woman is honest. Okay, can you rest your arm on your side? I'm going to clean this up a bit and make sure we're all sterile. Sterile as we can be."

Marissa opened her eyes. "It's going to hurt, isn't it?"

"You'll feel a sting."

She closed her eyes again. Alex thought she was magnificent and strong. He guessed maybe he'd been wrong about city girls. Some of them could hold their own.

Doc stitched her up and then he turned his attention to her wrist. Alex got mad all over again. Her wrist, small and fine-boned, was bruised and swollen.

"It's going to be sore for a few days," Doc told her as he wrapped it. "But I don't think anything is broken."

"Thank you. And I have insurance," Marissa offered.

Doc patted her shoulder. "This is on the house."

"Doc, you say that about ninety percent of the time."

"Yeah, well, I'm old and I can do what I want."

Doc stood and gave his patient another good look. "You'll be okay, just sore and maybe a little jumpy for a week or so. But you did a good thing getting that little girl to safety."

"I didn't think."

"Maybe not, but you did a good thing. Now try to rest. I'll have someone bring you a plate."

Doc left and Alex moved a little closer to Marissa. She was watching him, studying his face, and she looked concerned. He didn't want her to worry about him.

Before he could tell her that, someone rapped on the door. He called for them to enter and a head peeked in. Dan looked a little bit pale and his eyes were wild beneath the shaggy eyebrows.

"Where's my granddaughter?"

"Come in, Granddad. I'm fine. I promise." Marissa winked at Alex as she called out to her grandfather.

"You have visitors," Dan said as he pushed the door open. Alex wasn't sure about visitors. But little Julie and her mom, Trish, entered behind Dan.

"I wanted to thank you," Trish said as she got closer to the bed. "I don't know what would have happened if…"

Alex watched as Marissa held a hand out to the woman, but she made a very pointed look at Julie, and he agreed. The child didn't need to hear what might have happened.

"I'm just real grateful," Trish said as she pulled her daughter close. "Julie is really glad you were there, too."

"Me, too." Then Marissa held her arms open to the child.

Julie took cautious steps forward, eyeing the bandaged arm and the wrist that had been wrapped. "You'll be okay?"

"Of course I will. And you will, too. I promise."

"We won't keep you. We just wanted to say thank you." Trish took Julie by the hand and led her from the room.

"I had them make your plate to go," Dan said in a less gruff than usual manner. Alex had to take a second look to make sure it was the real Dan.

"I can drive you home," Alex offered.

"Trying to get rid of me?" Marissa asked, her expression soft.

That was a question he didn't want to answer. Not at the moment. It wasn't simple. He needed her to leave, before he couldn't let her go. He needed her to stay, but he knew she wouldn't.

Alex was in big trouble.

Chapter Fifteen

Sun was streaming through the window and Bub moved, pushing and trying to hog the couch Marissa slept on. She moved and an aching back and arm greeted her. After a few minutes she rolled to her side and Bub slid in a boneless heap to the floor.

The clock on the wall chimed eight times. Marissa shot off the couch, her legs shaking as she righted herself. It was long past time to feed the animals. How had she missed her alarm? And Red the rooster? Surely nothing had gotten the rooster. What if a coyote had found the nuisance bird?

She reached for her shoes and a sharp, stinging pain in her arm reminded her of the stitches. One sprained wrist and a stitched-up arm. Somehow she hadn't thought about what a detriment that would be to getting ready in the morning.

Actually, it would be a hindrance to the many things she needed to get done today. Not to mention playing the piano. The Christmas performance was a week away.

With great care she managed to slide on her shoes. As she stood back up, the door of the camper opened. Her grandfather gave her a look. He had the fireproof box in his hands and he sat it on the table.

"What are you doing up?" he asked.

"I overslept and I was going to go feed. What have you been doing?"

He reached for his oxygen tank and gave her a gloating look. "I'm taking care of my livestock the way I've been doing it for nigh on sixty years. And you should be resting after the day you had yesterday."

"I feel much better." Which wasn't really the truth. She had an arm in a sling and one wrist wrapped up.

"Sit down and I'll get you a cup of coffee. You've been taking care of me. Time I took care of you." He gave her a look and she sat.

"Why did you bring the box in?" she asked as he moved around the kitchen. She shivered a bit thinking of him climbing around alone in the barn.

"I'll show you in a bit." He pulled eggs from the fridge and set to cracking them in a bowl. "I know you thought I needed to be taken care of, but I'm pretty handy in the kitchen. And I have to admit that I feel better since I've started taking Doc's advice with the oxygen and your advice on eating healthier."

"You've complained a lot."

He shot her a grin. "Yeah, well, I've been complaining for a long time. It's habit."

"Why are we having this conversation?"

He poured eggs into a buttered skillet. "Well, I've been thinking that it's probably about time for you to head back to Dallas and I don't want you worrying, thinking I can't take care of myself. I know you have a job and friends. You have your parents. I don't want you staying here thinking that if you leave, something bad is going to happen. It won't."

"I know that." Or she hoped she did. But that didn't mean she wouldn't worry.

"You've got to get back to your life, honey." He stirred the eggs and then reached for the coffeepot. "I'm going to be blunt. I know I'm just an old man but I can see that a young woman like you would like Alex. He's a good kid, works hard, I guess he's not too ugly even if he does have those ears."

She laughed.

"But I've been down this road before. Your grandmother thought the same things about me.

She liked the idea of a cowboy and a ranch, until we was hitched and she had to move to Bluebonnet."

"I'm not planning on hitching myself to anyone, Granddad," she informed him. But saying the words out loud, she felt a sense of loss. If she left here, she'd leave so much behind. She would leave behind people and things she never would have known or missed if she hadn't come.

She wouldn't regret.

If she didn't go home, she'd let down her parents. She'd also let down the school that had hired her. She had a contract to fulfill.

Her grandfather turned off the stove and brought her a cup of coffee. A minute later he returned with eggs and toast.

"I'm going to miss you," he admitted in a softer voice than she'd heard from him before.

He scratched his chin, looked at her and walked off. His back was to her as he headed to the stove, but his hand came up and he swiped at his face.

"I'll be back. I promise," she assured him.

"I'm counting on that." He returned to his chair with a plate of eggs and toast. "And that's what the box is about."

"What's in the box?"

"Don't get yourself all worked up. I'll show you when I'm good and ready."

He turned on the news, as if he was enjoying dragging this out, making her wait. After he'd finished he took both plates to the sink and did the dishes. Marissa sat cross-legged on the couch, waiting for him to finish. She smiled and pretended it didn't bother her to be kept waiting. To illustrate that point, she picked up her phone and scrolled through emails and social media.

Eventually he returned to his chair, picking up the box on his way. He pulled a key out of his pocket and lifted the lid of the box. She couldn't see what it was that he sifted through, but his eyes had narrowed as he looked it all over.

"Well, I'll be. I'd forgotten some of this was in here."

"What is in the box?" she groaned, beyond tired of waiting.

Holding the box with one hand, he used the other to empty the contents, and he placed it all on the table next to his chair. Stacks of money, envelopes and papers.

"What is all of that?" She leaned to get a better look.

"My life savings. It isn't much, but enough to build a house with a couple of bedrooms and a nest egg for the future." He held up several official-looking documents. "I'd forgotten all about these stocks."

"What are they for?"

"Oh, some crazy idea of your grandmother's. She told me to invest in technology. That was twenty or thirty years ago. I guess it might be worth something now."

With a groan, Marissa fell back on the couch. "You think?"

His blue eyes twinkled merrily. "Yeah, I imagine. I'll have to check that out. Maybe the two of us can take a trip to Hawaii."

She sat up again, brushing her hair back from her face. "Not Hawaii. Maybe the Bahamas?"

"A cruise?"

"Yes," she said. "A cruise would be good."

Her phone rang. She gave her grandfather an apologetic look. "It's my mom."

"You go ahead and talk. I'm going to take care of a few things in the barn. I'm putting this box under my bed. I guess I should trust a bank with that cash and figure out what those stocks are worth."

"Hi, Mom," Marissa answered as her grandfather left the room. "How are you?"

"The question would be, how are you? Your grandfather called us this morning."

The traitor. "Oh, I see. I've been meaning to call. I'm going to be in the community Christmas program. I'd love for you all to come."

A long pause followed. Her mom cleared

her throat. "Yes, okay. And then can we bring you home?"

"Yes, of course." After all, she couldn't hide in Bluebonnet Springs forever.

They talked for several minutes. Afterward Marissa couldn't remember all that they'd talked about. Her brain was trying to wrap itself around the thought of leaving Bluebonnet…her grandfather.

And Alex.

Alex stood in the center of the arena and watched the filly at the end of the lunge line. She started to move in on him and he picked up the whip. That's all he had to do, show her. Her ears pricked forward and she moved back to the end of the line, keeping it tight.

"Walk," he said firmly.

She acted a bit like an impetuous toddler but she did what he asked. The early afternoon sun brushed her coat with gold. He couldn't help but feel a little proud of her. She was the offspring of his best mare and the sire belonged to a friend outside of Austin.

A truck pulled up to the barn. She did a startled little dance but he spoke to her and she settled. Her ears continued to twitch, though, as she sniffed for a hint of the newcomer.

"Easy," he said quietly. "Halt."

She stopped with her hooves squared up and her neck long. Yeah, she was going to be a champion.

"She's beautiful," Marissa called out from the side of the arena. "I thought you were mainly a fan of getting trampled by bulls."

He walked up to the filly, ran a hand down her golden-red neck, then whispered that she was still his favorite female. But he'd be parting with this four-legged favorite very soon. He had wanted to keep her but he was going to need to start liquidating assets so he could pay the mortgage before the auction could take place. He had a buyer looking at his bulls, too.

"I heard that," Marissa called out as she came through the gate. "A horse is your favorite female?"

Did the woman know nothing about boundaries? He led the filly across the arena. She kept an even pace, staying at his shoulder. A month ago she enjoyed nipping at him. Today she kept her teeth to herself.

"How are you doing today?" Alex asked.

"Better. Sore but I'm going to be fine. I wanted to thank you for yesterday."

"Thank me for what? If anything, I should have been there sooner."

"Don't," she warned. "Really, you couldn't have done anything. And I obviously did just fine."

He knew she was teasing but it didn't help. Not really. He felt responsible. Her hand touched his arm, stopping him from walking away. He glanced down at her and she looked up at him with eyes the color of a winter sky. Dark lashes fringed those amazing orbs and he couldn't help but get a little bit lost.

"I'm not sure why you feel as if you let me down. I think you might need to deal with that, with the idea that you should be able to rescue everyone in your life. We can't always rescue people. Sometimes they have to rescue themselves. And sometimes the circumstances are just so dire that we don't have the tools to do what is needed. I'm trying really hard to come to terms with the truth, that I didn't cause my sister's death. I made a bad decision. She made a bad choice to follow. But we were children. Were you ever a child, Alex?"

They were in the barn and he cross-tied the filly so he could brush her out. When she was secure he took Marissa by the hand and led her to the storage room. He opened the door and flipped on a light. He didn't go in.

"What?" she asked, clearly puzzled.

"This is the room my dad locked my sister in. For two days he kept her in there. He played Johnny Cash on a CD and ignored when she cried for him to let her out. After a while she stopped crying. I tried to bust her out but he must have known and he dragged me back to the house."

"I'm so sorry."

"My father was about the meanest man I've ever known. And that isn't something to be proud of. It isn't a legacy to keep going."

"You aren't like him, Alex," she said as she rubbed her hand down his arm. "You're nothing like him."

She pulled his head down and he rested his cheek against the top of her head. Her hand rubbed circles on his back and for the longest time he let her just hold him. He'd never told anyone outside the family, other than Pastor Matthews, about the storage room. He'd always worried what type of reaction he'd get if he shared.

This woman had a quiet strength. It seeped into him and he drank it up. He regretted that he'd met her, because now he would have to know what it felt like to lose her.

"Why are you here?" he asked as he held her close. He had a good idea what had brought her by. But he wanted to hear it from her.

"I wanted to visit."

"That's all?"

"And I wanted to tell you in person that I'll

be leaving after the community Christmas program Sunday."

"I see." He pulled back from her. Her gaze drifted from his.

"Dan is going to build a house."

"It's about time. Why is he going to build it now?"

"He said he needs an extra bedroom so I can visit from time to time. And I assured him I will be back. I'm also going to see if he'll come to Dallas for Christmas."

"I'm glad. He needs his family."

"We need him," she responded. "I should go so you can get back to work."

"Yeah, I have a tractor I need to get repaired before tomorrow."

Then everything was suddenly awkward and she backed away from him. "I'll see you soon?"

"Yes, soon. I don't know how much I'll see you between now and when you leave, but I'll definitely see you at the Christmas program and craft fair."

She stood on tiptoe and kissed his cheek. "I'm so glad you stopped and picked me up on the road."

He managed a half-hearted grin but couldn't agree. She had complicated his life. For the first time ever, he found himself wishing he could walk a woman down the aisle. He found himself wanting little girls with dark hair and blue eyes. But thinking those thoughts wouldn't get him anywhere.

She left and he went back to the filly, giving her a good brushing that had her nipping at his shoulder. Her way of pleading for him to stop already. He got the hint, so he tossed the brush in a bucket and untied her to lead her to the stall.

"Was that Dan's granddaughter leaving?" Maria asked as she entered the barn. He glanced her way and did a double take.

He couldn't quite put her in the box of annoying little sister when she looked like a college girl. Her hair was straight and not a tangled curly mess. She wasn't wearing jeans, boots and a T-shirt.

"What in the world are they doing to you down in Houston?"

Her hazel eyes narrowed at that question. "What is that supposed to mean? And don't think I'm forgetting about Dan's granddaughter being here with my brother."

"She came by to let me know she's leaving. So, back to you. Where are you going all dressed up like that?"

She spun in a slow circle, showing off the flowery dress. She was eighteen and his little sister. He wasn't exactly a father figure but she had been a little girl of eight when their dad died. He'd been looking out for her for a long time.

"I'm going on a date," she informed him with a secret smile.

"Are you? Is he picking you up here?"

"No, he isn't. I'm meeting him." She walked closer to him, smiling shyly, but he knew it was a ruse to get him off balance. "And I thought you should know, Marcus is home. He pulled in a few minutes ago and he's unloading his truck, like he plans to stay awhile."

"I'm not sure if that's good or bad. But about this date, why is he not picking you up here? Don't guys do that anymore?"

"No way would I let a guy come here. You're a ferocious pit bull when it comes to protecting your sisters. And you have such a bad opinion of marriage, you can't imagine why anyone would want to date or get serious."

"I don't have a bad opinion of…" He gave her a long look. "Are you thinking of getting marr—"

She cut him off. "Of course not. I have a lot of college ahead of me. I'm saying that because Marissa Walker just left and I'm guessing you're going to let her just walk away."

"Since it would be considered kidnapping if I kept her here against her will. Yes, I guess I am going to let her walk away. She has a job in

Dallas. I have a life here. She came here to meet her grandfather. She met him. Now she's going back to her home and her life."

"I love you, Alex, but you're as dense as Marcus when it comes to relationships."

"I heard that, and I resent it." Marcus stood in the doorway of the barn, looking a bit worse for wear.

"I'm being honest. Both of you are a mess. It's a good thing you all have me." She kissed Alex on the cheek and then danced out of his way and headed for the door.

"Go. And have fun. But be safe," Alex called out after her. "And don't fall for any sappy lines."

"Maybe you should learn some new lines," she said as she stopped just outside the door. He should have let her go. Instead he followed.

"You think?"

"Yeah, I think." She was all serious now. "It does wonders. We women like to think we're all strong and independent. But we still like to be told we're beautiful. We like surprises and flowers. We even like candlelight dinners."

He let her go without trying to get the last word. Besides, he had Marcus to contend with. As identical twins, he didn't think they shared any of that I-feel-what-you-feel bond. But Marcus was there. And hadn't he been thinking it would be good if his brother came home?

"Dan's granddaughter?" Marcus asked as he headed for the barn.

"What?" Alex grabbed a lead rope. He had a young gelding he wanted to green break before he sold him. If he could get the horse under saddle, he'd bring more money than he would barely halter broke. And he could use all the money he could make right now.

"Maria is giving you advice. I guessed it had something to do with Dan's granddaughter." Marcus stepped closer, making it easier to hear his words.

Alex didn't miss how his twin cast a nervous look around the barn, almost as if he expected their father to come roaring from a stall, prepared to beat him half to death. Rather than make Marcus talk, Alex filled the uneasy silence that hung between them.

"Yeah, Maria is convinced I'm in love. She's young. She doesn't get that we have other things on our minds."

"Such as?" Marcus asked.

"Saving this ranch. Whether we like it or not, it's ours."

"Put it on the market. I'll give you the money for the second mortgage if you'll sell the whole place."

"I don't want to put it up for sale. I want to live here."

Marcus shrugged. "Suit yourself. Get a loan. Borrow from Dane and Lucy, but my offer stands."

"It's a piece of land, Marcus. It isn't him. And I heard back from the bank. They won't give me a loan until the second mortgage is paid off and our mother signs the place over to us."

"I can't be here without hearing his voice. I can't listen to Johnny Cash without thinking about Lucy in that room. I don't want to save this ranch."

Alex wanted to be angry at his brother, but he got it. He understood. And he also realized Marcus wasn't as bad off financially as they all thought.

"I understand," he said, finally managing to get the words out.

Marcus nodded. "I know."

"How long are you staying?"

"Christmas." Marcus moved away from him but he stopped at the door. "I'll help you out. But then I'm done with this place."

Alex stood in the doorway of the barn watching his brother's stiff-legged walk as he headed to the house. Because when Alex had tried to humor and charm their father, Marcus had gone against him physically. And lost.

They were all on the losing end of this situation.

Chapter Sixteen

Marissa watched her mother as she helped her grandfather out of the back of her car. He didn't object the way he typically would. Instead he thanked her, then he turned to Marissa and winked.

"What should we do first?" she asked as she stepped to his side.

Her parents had shown up earlier in the day. To break the ice, her grandfather had gotten her dad talking about the house he wanted to build. That had kept the two men busy all day.

Her grandfather nodded in the direction of the craft booths. "I reckon I'd start over there with the crafts, baked goods and doodads you women seem to like. Me and Joe will head on over to the funnel cakes. I've got a hankering for something fried."

Her grandfather gave her a triumphant look

as he headed for the funnel cakes. She couldn't help but smile. He seemed a different man from the one she'd met when she'd first shown up.

As they walked, her dad matched his steps to her grandfather's and the two men talked as if they'd known each other for years, not days.

"This suits you," her mom said as they walked toward the craft booths.

Marissa looked up surprised. "Suits me?"

Her mom touched her hair. "Well, other than the hair. This town. Your grandfather. You seem happy."

Marissa glanced around, at the tents where tables were set up to sell crafts, desserts and other items. Children were playing in a bounce house. In less than an hour the churches would start the program. Two plays, several songs and the nativity story read by Pastor Matthews. The booth rentals, as well as money from the funnel cakes, would go to the shelter.

"I can't deny that I like it here," she admitted after some thought.

"I can see that," her mom acknowledged, pulling her close to hug her. "It's a comfortable place. I hadn't really thought about it a lot since I was a little girl. But I remember being happy here."

"It's a shame you never got to come back."

Her mom lifted one shoulder in an elegant but

casual gesture. "Yes, I guess it was a shame. I never thought too much about it. We left. I don't know why we left, but it happened. My mother came in one day and told me to pack a bag and hug my father goodbye. It must have been traumatic because I didn't think much about it until I came here to get you. That's when the memories rolled over me."

"I do love Granddad," she told her mother. "He took me in and even though he grumbled a bit, I knew from the start that he wouldn't want me gone."

"No, I can't suppose he would." Her mom reached for her hand. "And I owe you an apology. I've not been a good mother."

"We all did our best." But she really didn't want to talk about what had happened. Fortunately her mother seemed of the same mind and the conversation ended.

Marissa's gaze drifted over the crowd and landed on one person. Alex stood near his truck. He had the gray pony tied to the post of a round pen. A crowd of children had gathered for pony rides.

"You're not going to give everything up for a cowboy? Are you?" her mother asked as they walked to a craft booth with beaded jewelry.

She glanced past her mom and saw that Alex

was watching. Would it really be giving everything up? "Mom, I don't want to discuss this."

Discussing it would be pointless. Because she did have to leave, but she was leaving behind more than she'd ever expected. Her grandfather, Bea, Essie, Alex, even the animals. She'd come here to get over a failed attempt at a wedding and now she was going to have to get over being here.

But this she could come back to.

"I'm sorry," her mom said as the two of them looked over the jewelry. "I know that you have your own choices to make. I would just hate for you to give up everything on a whim."

She wanted to tell her mom that nothing she did was on a whim. If her mom knew her better, she would know that Marissa planned everything. She wouldn't walk away from those plans for fear of letting her parents down.

They were paying for their purchases when Pastor Matthews approached with a woman Marissa had seen at church but hadn't met. She smiled a greeting at the two as she and her mother started to move onto the next booth.

"Marissa, wait, if you don't mind." Pastor Matthews spoke quickly before Marissa could leave. "I have someone I want you to meet."

"I'm Theresa Wilkins, I'm the superintendent of the district school. I've heard so much about you and I was hoping, if you're planning on staying in the community, that we could sit down and talk."

"Talk?" Marissa gave her mom a worried glance, because this was probably the last thing her mom wanted to hear.

"About a job," Theresa continued. "We're a small school and we lose a lot of younger teachers to bigger schools, where there are more opportunities and better pay. We're looking for teachers who will be committed to our community and stay with us."

A job. Marissa couldn't help it, her gaze slid to where Alex led the pony, Cobalt, around the pen. A little boy was riding the pony and even from a distance appeared to be having the time of his life.

"I'm sorry, I already have a job."

"Well, if those circumstances should change, please call us."

"I will. Thank you."

Pastor Matthews and Theresa Wilkins left and Marissa returned to her mother's side. Neither of them mentioned the job opportunity. They made a few more purchases, then found their way to the music, where Marissa's father and grandfather waited. The two men had found chairs near the band and they were listening to music and finishing off a funnel cake.

"I have to go inside soon," Marissa said after a few minutes of uncomfortable silence. "I have to find Bea."

What she needed was a moment alone to think, and to maybe grieve the job offer she couldn't take. It was the job she had always wanted. As she made her excuses and walked away from the others, she thought about the fact that it wasn't forever. There would be other job openings in the future. Maybe someday she could return to Bluebonnet to live and to build a life for herself.

The halls of the church were quiet and as she walked, she prayed, something she hadn't done much of in her life. It felt foreign, to take those few moments and her worries and give them to God. It felt like whispering secrets into the dark as a child, hoping someone could hear.

"Marissa," a voice, strong and familiar, called to her from the end of the hall.

She spun around and faced Alex, plastering a shaky smile on her face. "Hey. I was afraid I wouldn't get a chance to tell you goodbye."

"It is goodbye then," he said as he drew closer, stepping out of the shadows. "I was hoping you would take Theresa's offer."

"You knew?"

"Well, yes. I told her you might be interested in a job. I wasn't sure."

She blinked away silly tears. For a few minutes she'd thought that she'd done this on her own. Someone had wanted her for her abilities and not her connections. It didn't really matter now. It wasn't as if she could take the job anyway.

"Of course," she said hesitantly because she didn't know what should come next. Her thoughts tumbled through her mind. She was hurt that the job hadn't really been about her skills, but hopeful because he wanted her to stay. Or maybe not. Maybe he'd just been helping her get what he thought she wanted.

"Marissa?"

She wanted to stay close to him. Even there, in the hallway, she didn't want to walk away. She wanted him to say something that mattered. But she was afraid of what he might, or might not say.

"I have to go find Bea," she said. "But thank you. I can't take the job. I already have one."

"Yes, I know."

As she walked away she thought he whispered that he would miss her.

Alex sat on the opposite side of the church from Marissa and her family. Lucy sat on one side of him. Maria sat on the other. As if they thought he needed their protection. To top it off, they kept giving him cautious looks, as if they thought he was falling apart.

He wasn't. He was pretty close to frantic, though. That wasn't what he'd expected to feel. It was the crazed feeling a person gets when they see someone about to drive away, and there was no way to stop them. He'd felt this way before, when their mother left the first time. She said she couldn't take it anymore and she'd gotten in a car and left.

From time to time she breezed back into their lives as if she hadn't crushed them as children. As if she hadn't let them down. Each time she'd left he'd wanted to chase after her and bring her back, because Maria had needed more than a maniac father and siblings who couldn't be a mother to her.

He hated the feeling.

He wanted to run from it, but not after the person leaving. Because he guessed if he ran after her, he would always be running after her, trying to convince her to stay. He started to get up but Maria put a hand on his arm.

He sat back down.

Bea had moved from the audience to the stage. A movement on the other side of the sanctuary caught his attention. He glanced at Marissa taking her seat at the piano. A hush fell over the crowd. Marissa began to play and then Bea's voice joined.

Throughout the sanctuary were surprised murmurs. People who hadn't seen Bea's last performance were in awe. He sat in awe of the woman at the piano. He couldn't help but remember the bedraggled bride, rain pouring down her face, threatening him with her high-heeled shoe. He grinned a little.

Maria elbowed him in the side.

"Don't be a moron," she whispered.

"Hush," he said.

"Don't let her go."

"Quiet," Lucy whispered. "But she's right."

"Not. My. Choice," he murmured.

Bea caught his attention again. She had moved to Marissa's side. They joined together singing "Carol of the Bells." He closed his eyes and drew in a steadying breath. Tonight the woman at that piano was going to leave town, walk out of his life, and he would miss her.

He didn't quite know what to do about it. Chase her car down the road like a scared kid? Beg her to stay?

No, he wouldn't do either of those. She had to make her own decisions about staying or leaving. She had to want to be in Bluebonnet. For now she'd made her decision. She'd chosen Dallas.

He had things to focus on. He had his own stuff to take care of. The auction was a week away. He was running out of time.

What could he offer Marissa? Not much, he guessed.

After the program ended he spotted her talking to a group of people. She saw him and he told himself it was happiness that lit up her face and that he had something to do with that happiness. She excused herself and headed his way.

"I wanted another chance to say goodbye," he told her.

"I'm glad." She took his hand in hers. "I'm so glad you found me on the side of the road that day."

"Would it be wrong to say that I'm glad Aidan picked the caterer instead of you?"

She laughed at that. "I think I'm kind of glad, too."

"I'm trying to do more than say goodbye."

"Don't." She leaned close to him. "It'll hurt too much. I have to go. My parents… I feel like I've spent a lifetime letting them down and if I don't go home, I'll be letting them down again."

"I'm not going to beg you to stay, but I would like to see you again. I'll drive to Dallas. Or if you're here visiting Dan."

"I would like that." She kissed his cheek. "I have to go now."

It sounded like goodbye in more ways than one. More of a "we'll do lunch" than an "I really want you in my life."

Her hand pulled free from his and he stood there watching her walk away. Who knew a city girl in a wedding dress could change his life and everything he'd thought he wanted? But she had and he knew if she didn't come back, he would miss her forever.

Chapter Seventeen

A pounding on his door woke Alex. He rubbed
at his face and crawled off the couch he'd slept
on. The pounding continued.

"I'm coming," he yelled.

He yanked the door opened and there stood
Dan. "It took you long enough."

"It's six in the morning." Alex opened the
door a little wider and motioned the older man
inside.

"I figured you'd be up early selling off some
livestock."

It was late January and he had gotten an ex-
tension. The ranch would be auctioned off on the
first of February unless he could come up with
all of the money. He'd already sold his bucking
bulls. It had been easy, hadn't felt at all like letting go of a dream.

"Yes, I'm selling livestock. Later." He headed

for the kitchen and the coffeepot and let Dan trail along behind. "What has you out of bed so early?"

He poured water in the coffee maker. Marcus entered the kitchen looking like a long-haired bear that had come out of hibernation.

Dan glanced at Alex's twin. "Good grief, you don't wear that hair in one of them man-buns, do you?"

Marcus gave Dan a narrow-eyed look and practically growled. He went to the fridge and poured himself a glass of juice. "What's he doing here?"

"I'm here to do what you haven't done. Help your brother." Dan pulled a checkbook out of his back pocket.

"I helped," Marcus grumbled.

"Dan, I don't want your money."

Dan didn't respond. He wrote out a check and slid it across the table. "Don't be prideful. You didn't get yourself into this mess. If you had, I wouldn't help. You've helped me a lot over the years. Not once have you asked to be paid, you just helped. I got to figuring up what I should have paid you and it came to quite a sum."

"Dan, you can't do this."

Dan held up a hand. "I found some good stuff in that old lockbox. Let's just say, I'm not going to worry too much about my future. And neither is my granddaughter. You remember her, don't you? Pretty little thing with dark hair and blue eyes."

From the kitchen table, Marcus snickered. Alex shot him a warning look.

"I remember your granddaughter, Dan." Alex lifted the coffeepot. "Want some?"

"Nah, I don't have time for that. Go pay off the mortgage and buy this ranch before your mother pulls another stunt."

Marcus picked up the check and whistled. He handed the check to Alex.

"I can't take that."

Dan slid it back to him. "You can. And you will. I'm making an investment. In your future. And I hope in the future of my granddaughter."

"How will this money help her future?" Alex asked, but then he got it. And obviously Marcus got it because his rusty-sounding laugh echoed as he left the room.

"School gets out early today," Dan said with meaning.

"Okay?"

"That gives you time to do your chores, clean up and get on the road." Dan patted the check. "Investment in the future. I wouldn't want you going through life deep in debt. I'd rather give you a gift than an inheritance."

"Dan, you don't have to do this."

Dan pushed to his feet. "Follow me. I have to show you something."

Out of curiosity, Alex followed Dan outside. He was surprised to see his sister Maria standing by his truck.

"What are you doing here?" he asked.

"Dan called and asked if I would help him out." She opened the passenger door of this truck. "Everything you need."

"Because you don't seem to be able to do this on your own," Dan said in his typical gruff tone.

Inside his truck was a box with a necklace, a book of poetry and a bouquet of flowers. "What do you want me to do with all of this?" he asked his sister.

"Go to Dallas and get a girlfriend," Maria said. "I know you thought she'd leave and after a while you'd forget her, but you're not. Forgetting her, that is. And so I'm helping you with romance. Because women do like it. Even strong, independent women. It's how we're made. And so you need to do something romantic."

"I'm not going to Dallas."

"Think about it. Please. I'll take all of this stuff to the house and then it's up to you."

"You can take it inside or take it back to the store. It doesn't matter to me."

She punched his arm. "Why are you being so stubborn?"

He stopped, let out a sigh and thought about how he'd almost believed she was no longer his annoying little sister. "I'm stubborn because it's how we've always survived. I haven't heard from her since she left. So what I'm assuming is she came here, had fun with a cowboy and went back to her real life."

"Idiot. Have you contacted her since she left?"

No, but he wasn't going to admit that.

She punched him again.

"Stop doing that." He rubbed his arm.

"I just wanted to make sure I had your attention."

"You have it. Now I have to feed livestock. If you want to help, get out of those city clothes and put on your work clothes."

"I'd love to help, but I'm going to lunch with Lucy." She headed for the house with the flowers, necklace and book of poetry.

"You're still a nuisance," he shouted after her.

Dan cleared his throat, reminding Alex of his presence and his part in this whole plot. "She's trying to help. So am I. I saw Marissa at Christmas. She didn't miss that idiot that walked out on her. She does miss you. And if I'm guessing correctly, you miss her. I know I made a lot of comments about tying yourself to a city girl, but I was wrong. And you were wrong to let her go."

"It isn't just because she's from the city, Dan.

What am I supposed to offer her? A ranch in debt. A past that makes me question what kind of husband and father I'll be? I can give her all the flowers in the world but it isn't going to make up for all that."

Dan rolled his eyes to heaven. "I can't believe you're going to make me say this. You're not Jesse Palermo. You're not even a close second. You've been like a grandson to me. If you were anything like your father, I would have run you off years ago."

"Thanks, Dan."

"Don't thank me. And I guess don't let me make you do something you don't want to do."

Alex nodded in agreement and Dan left, heading back to his place in his old farm truck. Alex thought about the check on his table and he thought about that old farm truck that Dan would drive until it fell apart.

But then his thoughts shifted to Marissa.

He wasn't taking a woman a book of poetry.

But he might take her flowers and a necklace. Because he might give himself one last chance. Stubbornness might not be the best trait to have in a relationship. And if a relationship was what he wanted with Marissa, he guessed he might need to work on that. Some women were worth chasing after. Especially if they need a little help realizing a man really loved them.

He loved her.

He shook his head at the thought because it wasn't what he'd expected that day he helped a rain-soaked bride into his truck. But it had happened.

Marissa watched the last of her students get on the bus. Her friend and co-teacher, Laura, stood next to her. Laura let out a sigh.

"I'm so glad this week is over. Is it spring break yet?"

Marissa shook her head. "No, but I wish it was."

"Big plans?" Laura asked as they headed back inside.

"Not really. I think I might go visit my grandfather."

At the thought of returning to Bluebonnet Springs, her heart kicked up a notch. She'd missed being there. She missed her grandfather. She missed Essie's café, the church and, most of all, she missed Alex.

There were days she thought she'd call, and then she thought maybe he was happy with the way things had ended. She wanted to tell him that she wasn't renewing her contract at this school. She'd already explained to her parents that it was time she made a few decisions for herself. And she couldn't teach here. Didn't want to teach here. She wanted a school like the one at Bluebonnet because she wanted to teach children like the ones who lived at the shelter. She wanted to inspire them to dream and to believe they could make a difference.

Thinking about Bluebonnet made her want to go sooner than spring break. Maybe today. She could be there in a few hours, spend the long weekend at her grandfather's and be back Monday night in time for school Tuesday.

"You've gone all gooey," Laura said.

"What?"

Laura laughed. "We were talking about spring break and you suddenly had this dreamy look on your face. And I don't think it was your grandfather you were thinking about."

"No, I wasn't." She glanced at her watch. "I'm going to Bluebonnet. I'll be back Tuesday."

"Have a good weekend," Laura said as Marissa hurried off.

She grabbed her purse and book bag from her office as she called her mom to let her know she wouldn't be coming home. She prepared herself for something less than understanding and was surprised when her mom told her it was about time.

She was pulling onto the main road when a truck came up behind her, headlights flashing. She glanced at the tailgater but kept driving. Soon the truck began to honk and the lights flashed again. She took another look in the rearview mirror and her heart collided with her ribs. She pulled to the shoulder of the road and got out of her car.

The truck pulled in right behind her. Alex took his time getting out. She stood near the back of her car. Traffic slowed to watch.

Finally he got out of the truck, his arms full. Flowers, a book, a box. She took a few steps toward him, toward his familiar presence. She'd missed him so much it had hurt, and now, seeing him, the hurt magnified because she didn't want him to go away.

"You almost missed me." She said it out of the blue. "I was leaving town."

"Were you?" he asked, awkward with his arms full. She should help him out but she didn't. He was too cute, too boyish, standing there with his gifts and that awkward, unsure look on his face.

"Yes, I was going to Bluebonnet Springs. I have friends there. I've missed them."

"Have you?" He moved his arms, trying to arrange things. "You could help a guy out. Maria insisted I should come prepared to romance you back into my life. Your grandfather helped her."

"Is that what this is?" She took the flowers. He managed then to get a hold of the box and the book. "What else do you have? Because I do like gestures. Grand gestures."

"I have a necklace." He managed to get it out of the box. "I'd like to say I had the forethought to pick it out. But Maria gets the credit."

He put the single teardrop diamond around her neck.

"Maria has good taste," Marissa told him.

"Yes, she does. She likes you." He opened the book of poetry.

She had to stop him. "Please, no poetry. I don't think I can handle that."

"Good, because I didn't really want to read poetry."

"I've missed you," she said as he stepped close, his nearness making it difficult to breathe.

"I know."

"You're supposed to say you missed me, too."

He took the flowers and held them to his side, and then he kissed her. It was a sweet, searching kiss. Cars driving past honked. Marissa didn't care. She kissed him back and then she rested her head on his shoulder.

"Are you sniffing me?" he asked.

"I am," she admitted. "I've missed every bit of you, even your scent."

"Will you please come back to Bluebonnet?" he asked with a voice that shook.

She was glad he wasn't altogether calm. She wanted to know that she wasn't in this alone.

"I told you, I was on my way there. I have a long weekend."

"I don't want you in Bluebonnet for a weekend. I want you there for good. In my life."

"O-o-h-hh," she said, drawing out the word.

He stepped back, returning the flowers to her hands. "Don't make me have to read poetry."

"Never," she promised.

"I'm not good at this. I'm not a man who ever thought he'd find someone he wanted to spend his life with. But I'd chase after you, Marissa. I'd do my best to never disappoint you."

"I'm coming back to Bluebonnet," she told him. "I'm taking a job at the local school. I'm also going to date a cowboy."

"Really? A cowboy?" He grinned, then lifted her off her feet and spun her around. "You are talking about me, right?"

When he set her back on her feet, she kissed him. "Yes, you're the only cowboy in my life."

"I plan on keeping it that way," he promised.

He followed her back to Bluebonnet Springs and as she drove into town it felt like a homecoming in more ways than one. The man she loved was behind her and their future was ahead of them.

Epilogue

It seemed fitting that Alex and Marissa would wait a year and have a Christmas wedding in Bluebonnet Springs. Marissa stood in the fellowship hall of the church as her mom made the last adjustments to her hair and veil.

"You look beautiful," her mom told her as she kissed Marissa on the cheek. "You were right, this dress is perfect."

Marissa looked in the mirror, pleased with what she saw. She kept her hair shoulder-length now but it had been pinned up with tendrils curling loosely around her face. The veil hung just to her neck. The dress was slim-fitting white velvet and with few adornments.

"Mom, thank you. For loving me. And for being here today."

"I think I'm more here than I've been in a very

long time," Mary told her daughter. "I'm sorry that it took so long."

Marissa hugged her mom. "No regrets. Let's just live the best life we can from this day forward."

"Yes, from this day forward." Her mom dabbed at her eyes. "From this day forward you will be Marissa Palermo. No longer my little girl, but a wife. And someday a mother."

"Stop. You'll make me cry."

"That'll make three of us," Maria said as she sashayed close in her dark red velvet bridesmaid's dress. "Your dad is at the door. It's almost time. Lucy is ready, too."

Her bridesmaid and her matron of honor. It was a simple wedding and Marissa couldn't have been happier. She kissed her mother's cheek one last time before she left to go find her seat in the church. And then Marissa walked out the door and took hold of her father's arm.

They walked around the building to the front of the church. Christmas lights twinkled in the shrubs on either side of the door. From inside she could hear Bea singing a song about forever. Marissa's dad patted her arm and then he led her up the steps and through the doors. She watched as her bridesmaids and groomsmen made their way down the aisle. And then her flower girl, Dane and Lucy's daughter, Lily, followed. She tossed flower petals in the air with gleeful giggles that Marissa had informed everyone was perfect. The child couldn't see, but she knew the number of steps to the front of the church and then Lucy would be there to guide her.

Bea's song ended. She laughed and said that she was so happy that Alex had been so neighborly to her friend Marissa, because now they were going to be a husband and wife. And wasn't that just the cat's meow. Soft laughter rippled through the congregation.

The wedding march began and Marissa's dad walked her down the aisle to the man of her dreams. A man she might have missed out on if her last groom hadn't left her for the caterer.

She knew that sometimes things happened for the very best reasons. The man standing at the front of this church was God's plan for her life.

Alex was her forever groom. And she was his Christmas bride.

* * * * *

Dear Reader,

I really wasn't sure what would happen to Alex Palermo when he found a bride on the side of the road. Who finds a bride? A person might find a puppy or a kitten, or maybe a stranded traveler, but never a bride. And when one finds a bride, what does one do with her? In Alex Palermo's case, stay as far away as possible. Unfortunately, circumstances made avoiding the pretty bride a difficult thing to do. In the case of Alex and Marissa, the lesson of "when God closes one door, another opens up" suddenly makes sense. When we think everything is falling apart, sometimes the plan is actually coming together for good.

Brenda

Get 2 Free Books,
Plus 2 Free Gifts—
just for trying the Reader Service!

Get 2 Free Books,

Love Inspired HISTORICAL

Plus 2 Free Gifts—

just for trying the
Reader Service!

Get 2 Free Books,
Plus 2 Free Gifts—
just for trying the
Reader Service!

◆HARLEQUIN

HEARTWARMING™

HW17R